Praise for *Running on Rooftops*

Running on Rooftops is a poignant fictional memoir about fortune and misfortune, love and tragedy, togetherness and aloneness. With her vivid, right-there-with-you prose, Andrea L. Stout serves up Tibetan yak milk, an eight-course Chinese wedding banquet—and the stark contradictions inherent to being young and foreign. It's a book for all humans, one that will inevitably leave you changed.

Kate Mueser,
author of *The Girl with Twenty Fingers*

Running of Rooftops

ANDREA L. STOUT

A Blackwater Press book

First published in the United States of America by
Blackwater Press, LLC

Library of Congress Control Number: 2025941508

ISBN: 978-1-7357747-5-6

Cover design by Eilidh Muldoon

Blackwater Press
120 Capitol Street
Charleston, WV 25301
United States

blackwaterpress.com

MIX
Paper
FSC® C100212

To the memory and legacy of my story-loving grandparents,
Med & Harriet Larson and Cal & Harriet Stout

ACKNOWLEDGMENTS

I began this novel as a graduate student, living in Glasgow, Scotland. By that time, I had already spent three years living and traveling across different regions of China, as well as making the occasional trip down into Southeast Asia. As an American, I had also lived in five different U.S. states. My move to Glasgow, then, at age thirty-one, became my third country of residence and my ninth overall "home" city. During the course of my graduate school writing and research, first for a master's degree in Creative Writing and then for a PhD in English Literature, the topic of expatriation and its representation in literature—with a particular focus on West-to-East expatriation literature—felt a natural one for me to pursue. A draft of this novel was one of the ensuing results.

After completing my graduate studies, I took a professorship in Hong Kong, teaching literature, writing, film, and general storytelling principles to students in creative fields. I remained there over four academic years until the COVID-19 pandemic forced a closure of my institution's campus, along with the closure of many borders, including the ones I was surrounded by. It was at this time, amidst my daily wanderings around Hong Kong's various island hills with no idea of where or when I might find myself next relocating, that I was approached (virtually) by a former University of Glasgow colleague and encouraged to revisit this novel for publication.

Since that initial "Let's bring this novel into the light of day" conversation, I have moved several more times, including to Indonesia and two different cities in Morocco (one of which is now my current location), in addition to the times of respite and safe haven I have found with my always open-armed family in Brush Prairie, Washington. The development of this novel, then, like life, has been quite the journey, and there are countless people across the world and throughout the years who have played a role in the creation of its story. Here, then, I would like to offer my humblest thanks to, and appreciation for, the following influences in my life and work.

First, I am indebted to the team at Blackwater Press for helping to bring this novel into the world in such a beautiful and tangible way. Blackwater's co-founder, Elizabeth Ford, the former University of Glasgow colleague of mine who contacted me during my Hong Kong pandemic isolation months, saw potential in my work from the beginning and had both the vision and the gumption to make it happen. It has been a true inspiration to see the ethos she has created and cultivated over at Blackwater in just a handful of years, and I'm honored to be a very small part of it. Particularly with regard to the development of this novel, I also cannot overstate the vital contribution of editor Vivien Williams. She has stuck with me through moves, job changes, life changes, schedule changes, and all manner of manuscript changes, ever patiently yet persistently helping to bridge the gaps in understanding between writer and reader. Thank you, Vivien, for helping to bring these characters to life. Occasionally, the edits felt a bit like therapy sessions, but, in the end, we have some feelings! Additionally, I would be remiss in not mentioning the oh-so-talented artist behind this cover, Eilidh Muldoon. Thanks to her, we all get to see some gorgeous rooftop views with just a simple reach to the bookshelf. Thank you for sharing your creativity, Eilidh.

Unending gratitude also goes to all of the incredible teachers I have had throughout my academic journey. In particular, I owe a world of thanks to my writing and literature professors back in Oregon, Colette Tennant and Jim Hills. They told an eighteen-year-old, soccer-playing college freshman with an undeclared major that she was a good writer, and with that they helped forever direct my course. Over the span of the next four years, they invested in me, not just as a student and a writer, but as a person, and their words, wisdom, and mentorship have lasted me my lifetime. Thank you, Dr. Tennant and Prof. Hills, for sharing your passion and showing us how to engage, empathetically and intelligently, with the beauty and the mess of humanity through the art of storytelling.

I also had the great fortune of being surrounded by a number of passionate and thoughtful writers during my grad school years at the University of Glasgow. To my workshop groups, fellow classmates, and friends who were always game to meet for a pint or a cuppa for brainstorming sessions or a simple break to leave the flat in order to stave off insanity: thank you for your gifts of time, mindfulness, and perspectives. I look forward to reading all of your future stories, as well. And particular thanks to my two stellar supervisors during this time: Elizabeth Reeder and Zoë Strachan. Their insights and feedback on the early iterations of each component of this story were invaluable. Thank you for scrutinizing everything from character development to verb tense choice with me and for encouraging me to "just keep going." It cannot be overstated just what a mental and emotional roller coaster it is trying to survive a master's degree, a PhD candidacy, sitting the viva, revising a thesis, and venturing out into the post-doctorate job hunt over the duration of six years, so thank you for knowing when to push and when to cheer.

I could go on for pages, recounting all the people who have befriended and supported me throughout my global wanderings, but, for brevity's sake, allow me to instead thank the various communities who have taken me in to their "pack of the packless": friends and colleagues in and around Changchun, Duilong and Lhasa, Nanning, Yinchuan, North Fort Myers, San Dimas and Pasadena, Fort Collins, Glasgow, Hong Kong, Papua, Fez, and Ifrane. And, of course, thanks always to my "hometown" crews of Brush Prairie, Portland, and Salem for always welcoming me back, ready to hear and share stories year after year.

Lastly, to my big, close-knit, story-loving family. I often joke that I grew up on a compound—though, thankfully, not the no-outsiders-allowed-and-you-can-never-leave kind—and it has provided me with many a fun conversation starter. From growing up with raccoons and possums for pets to summers of catch-and-releasing crawdads and frogs to building bridges and all manner of forts, the Family Farm has provided inspiration and adventure for generations, and I am so thankful to my grandparents, aunts and uncles, cousins, parents, siblings, siblings-in-law, and nieces and nephews for making it the magical setting that it is. For a habitual expat, what a gift it is to have a supportive family who are always there to cheer you on, visit your new adoptive country, and provide clean sheets and your favorite meal when you wander back home. Thanks especially to my parents, Steve & Nancy Stout, my Aunt Jane, and siblings and siblings-in-law: Steph & Jason, Ty & Sarah, and Jake & Christa—always my first test readers and loudest supporters; and to my nieces and nephews: Clover, Sydney, Toby, Jules, Med, Addie, Wavey, Leon, Melia, Riley, Zoe, and

Ike—for keeping me young and reminding me how to view the world with hopeful wonder.

A theme that often crops up in expatriate literature is the idea that, though living under a foreign sky often brings with it a newfound sense of freedom, without a place to belong and something to which to tie ourselves, it also brings with it the fear of being lost. So, thank you, friends, family, and mentors, for being those much-needed hitching posts throughout my life, travels, and sojourns—you allow me to wander without fear.

To be alive at all is to have scars.
—John Steinbeck

PROLOGUE

~ *Remembering The Future* ~

The most painful state of being is remembering the future, particularly the one you'll never have.
—Søren Kierkegaard

Hilo, Hawaii, July 2019—Another Fourth of July at the bay has come and gone, a tradition now six years running. Six years of standing outside amidst members of my adopted community, gazing up at the night sky, watching fireworks explode out over the water. Six years of life back in America … not actually North America but "the United States of," at any rate. Six years of belated graduate school after a decade of expatriate life across various Asian countries. And now, with a couple of additional degrees hanging on the wall back inside my apartment and the surrounding shelves spilling over with books and journals, crammed to the margins with descriptions of places and various esoteric scholarly ideas, here I am again, turning to the night sky for answers, wondering, as always, what comes next.

I know I should be celebrating beyond just a moment of rockets'-red-glare patriotism. I should, in fact, be commemorating having just completed this final degree. Now I can go, continue on with my life of traveling, writing, teaching, observing the world. But, to be honest, this part always feels unnerving, no matter how many times I've gone through it before. Staring out at this open expanse is at once a freedom and a burden—like an astronaut, I imagine, who stands at the ship's door, preparing to take that first step out into their next spacewalk, ready to be set adrift…but, still, triple-checking the tether. Endless, exciting worlds lie ahead, ready to be explored, but somewhere, always in the back of one's mind, a single, nagging thought remains: What if this is the time the cord breaks? What if this is the time of no return?

I should know better, though. As a child of the '80s, it's always a mistake to start thinking in terms of astronaut metaphors. Maybe watching the *Challenger* explode on live TV at such a formative age means one can't help but conjure up space exploration at times such as this. A new step forward will always mean an equal possibility of joy and grief. If I didn't understand that as a kid, I certainly do now. It could be that I've been reading too much from the Lost Generation lately—this most recent degree was a PhD researching expatriate literature, after all—but I think there's something to Fitzgerald's sentiment about being able to hold two opposing ideas in mind simultaneously. In fact, the more experiences one goes through, the more one probably begins to realize that most of what we've believed to be opposites actually aren't even necessarily dissimilar. I can believe both that, tomorrow morning, as I hand in the final edits of my dissertation at age thirty-eight, I am about to embark on my best-yet journey and also that the safety line is just about to snap. Either way, tonight I will hold these two opposing views in mind: I will both celebrate and mourn, raising a glass in cheer while also pouring one out, if not for myself, then for those gone before.

Likewise, maybe before heading off down this new path, I need to first look back, to examine those beginning steps fifteen years ago that set me on the course on which I now find myself—this life of bouncing around from place to place, from encounter to encounter, never at rest, never certain of a hold. It is a story born of colliding paths, of false steps and ensuing scars, but maybe, in the telling of it, I'll be able to find something running through, something to give clarity and meaning to an otherwise seemingly tenuously related series of chance meetings and twists of fate. Or, if there is no clarity nor meaning to be found, then at least I would like to be reminded of beauty, the kind of beauty best demonstrated by lives lived fully, youthfully, jumping headlong uninhibited into the unknown. This, then, is where I will begin: putting down onto paper the pieces of a year, the people, the places, the conversations without obvious purpose, trying to find a connection, and hoping at last to arrive at some kind of peace.

PART ONE

~ *EAST* ~

CHAPTER ONE

~ Becoming A Stranger ~

Oregon, May 2003—*A year. Perfect,* I thought as I picked up one of the pamphlets off the table. The tri-fold display, like all of the other college career fair banners and boards coloring the gym, seemed to be shouting at me: HAVE AN IMPACT. SEE THE WORLD. GAIN VALUABLE EXPERIENCE. But the detail that had caught my eye was that one, listed among the bullet points across the bottom: A one-year commitment. The Navy, giving out bumper stickers three booths down, was making a similar pitch, but it wanted four years in return. Four years. I was just finishing that with this degree, getting my bachelor's, studying literature and writing, and playing soccer. I had enjoyed it, but I wanted a break from long-term thinking. I just wanted a year to see what else was out there. The Navy or grad school or whatever else my future held could wait. Plus, hadn't my favorite authors, who wrote the most authentically about life, first gone out and experienced it? I folded the pamphlet and put it in my pocket.

* * *

Three months later, I was boarding a plane for China.

The fact that I had left family and friends and everything I knew to be home hadn't really sunk in during the Portland to Vancouver flight, but now, finding myself in this ten-seat-across impossibly large aircraft filling steadily with foreign dialects, I finally had an inkling just how different this next year might turn out to be. Other than one family vacation spent in Mexico, I had never felt so conspicuously out of place.

Newly inspired, or perhaps in an effort to stave off panic, I reached into my bag and pulled out my Mandarin Chinese phrasebook before tucking the rest of my things into the overhead bin and taking a seat. I'd tried to learn some of the basics after getting my school placement from the ESL agency seven weeks earlier, but admittedly, not much had stuck. Nevertheless, it was to be a twelve-hour flight—at least I could feel proactive.

"A friendly face, thank goodness."

I looked up to see a blond-haired, fifty-something woman standing in the aisle outside my row, smiling down at me. I stood to let her in, and after she had moved past me, she plopped down in the middle seat next to mine and let out a dramatic sigh.

"You'd hardly guess we were still in North America, would you?"

She unpacked a few items into her seatback pocket, then took a sip of her bottled water and dabbed the beads of sweat off her nose and forehead with a tissue.

Glancing at my phrasebook, she added, "Oh, good for you. I can't speak a word of Chinese and probably wouldn't make it two steps in the country by myself. But, of course, my son speaks it fluently—he's been over there eight years, working for one of these big companies—so I'll count on him to get me around."

She paused briefly as she watched an elderly Chinese couple take their seats in the row across from us. "And what about you? You look awfully young to be traveling to China on your own."

"I'll be teaching English for a year," I said. I'd been saying that a lot lately, trying to get used to the idea. As for the comment about looking young, I'd always been told that it was an inherited Scandinavian thing—red hair, freckles, rosy cheeks, and a youthful appearance for which I'd be thankful when I was older. "It's my first time living abroad," I added.

The woman nodded. "Now's the time to do it, when you're young. And they certainly pay well, don't they?"

As with everything else about this job—living overseas and teaching—having a salaried position was another first, so I wasn't sure if the money would be considered well-paying or not. But since the school would be providing my housing, it certainly seemed enough for a recent college graduate. Not knowing how to respond, I gave a sort of noncommittal "Mmm" by way of answer.

"Uh huh," she said, giving me a look as though the two of us were co-conspirators in some sort of elaborate money-making scheme. Lowering her voice, though still speaking too loud for my comfort, she added, "They all want to learn English, don't they? But I guess if they can afford it, why not?"

"I guess," I said, fidgeting with my phrasebook. I studied the illustration on the cover—a drawing of a Chinese woman holding a cup of tea—and wondered if it would help to open it.

"Who knows," the woman continued, sounding as though she were picking up some previously-held conversation, "you might even end up staying longer than a year. I'm sure my son never thought he'd stay over there as long as he has, but he's done quite well. And, of course, he's got himself a girlfriend—a *Eurasian*, half Chinese, half Irish, if you can imagine—but very pretty, from what I can tell from pictures. And they've just had a baby, so I don't know if he'll ever come back now. But that's why I'm visiting: because if I waited for Mark to bring my grandbaby home, I might never meet him."

She paused while digging through her handbag, then brought out a picture.

"Cute," I said when she flashed it toward me.

She smiled, then looked at the picture herself. "He looks very Asian, doesn't he?" She sounded more contemplative than anything else. "Very small eyes. But he's got my son's cheekbones, and I think the Irish is going to start showing up in the hair."

I watched the flight attendant pull the thick door to the outside shut and lock it with a push down on the handle. The woman beside me had moved on to the topic of Chinese names, and I prepared myself for the long flight.

***

After a sedentary day of air travel, arriving in the Beijing airport felt like someone had suddenly switched the reel into double time. Keeping the pace, I moved with the crowd through customs and then diligently followed the arrows pointing me toward my gate. I arrived with a few minutes to spare and took the closest empty chair, hoping to catch my breath before the next boarding.

"You are going to Yinchuan?"

This time I knew it wasn't a blond grandmother addressing me. Instead, I looked up to see a Chinese man, business-suited, perhaps in his thirties or forties. He was sitting one empty chair away from me but now got up and moved a seat closer.

"Yinchuan?" I repeated uncertainly. *Yin-chwon.* I realized I'd never heard it pronounced before, but yes, this was, indeed, where I was going: a city in the province of Ningxia, a two-hour flight west of Beijing, somewhere south of Mongolia and hemmed in by the Gobi Desert. This is what I had learned from looking at a map, anyway, after I'd been given my assignment. I nodded.

He had turned his attention to his cell phone, and I wondered if he had asked the question simply to confirm that he was at the right gate. Though why he would have asked me, of all people, for any kind of information involving the Beijing airport, I had no idea. I could see with one quick glance around that, among the fifty or so other passengers awaiting this flight, I was the only Caucasian.

"It is very remote," he said after taking another few moments to finish his text. "You are going for business or travel?"

"Business, I guess. I'll be teaching English."

He nodded at that but gave a slight frown. "Teachers are very good; we must learn English. But why do you go to Yinchuan? It is very small and poor. Beijing is better, or Shanghai or Guangzhou—you will make much more money, and I think it is more modern and comfortable for you."

"The college is in Yinchuan," I said. Debating whether I should try to defend my soon-to-be-adopted city with information I had read online or to explain that it was really no choice at all, I settled for adding, "I'm sure it will be fine. My hometown is small, too." In fact, from what I had read about Yinchuan, I knew that it was more than a hundred thousand people larger even than Portland, Oregon, which is what we considered the "big city" back home.

"Yes, very small," the man said, clearly unconvinced. "My business goes there only for the aluminum. I advise you to work in Beijing, instead. How long you will stay in China? You have a contract?"

"Yes," I said. "My contract's for a year …"

Just then, the door to the jetway opened, and the businessman stood up.

"Very good," he said, handing me a business card. "The Muslim food is very famous in Yinchuan. I hope you enjoy. Warmly welcome you to China."

And with that he joined the group pushing toward the gate.

A bit disoriented by the abruptness and unclear purpose of the exchange, I got slowly to my feet and walked to the back of the small crowd preparing to board. Whatever awaited me, there was no turning back now.

* * *

"Anne Henry?" a young, neatly-dressed Chinese woman greeted me as I stepped through security. She held a sign with my name on it, which seemed a gesture largely for my benefit as there seemed no one else in the airport for whom I could be mistaken. "I am Rose, from the university," she said, offering her business card. "Pleased to meet you. I have come to collect you."

I reciprocated the greeting, sans business card, and, as we waited for my luggage at the nearby belt, I expressed my gratitude for her being there, though relief was probably a more fitting description. It dawned on me that I'd never actually been in direct contact with anyone from the school and would not have known how to instruct a taxi or how to pay for a ride to the university if someone hadn't come to get me. The agency had made all of the arrangements.

Taking one of my two bursting-at-the-seams wheeled duffle bags, Rose led me outside to a sleek, black car waiting at the curb. The driver, standing in the shade of the building, put out his cigarette and stepped to the trunk to lift in my luggage without a word. I followed Rose as she slid into the backseat, and a moment later we set off. It would be a half-hour drive to the campus—another snippet of information I remembered from my city research.

Continuing our now mobile orientation, Rose began telling me more about her role at the university. In short, as Assistant Director of Foreign Affairs, she was to be my contact for everything, a sort of hand-holder, apparently. "Even if you need some help ordering in a restaurant, please call me," she said.

She reminded me of the hotel concierges I'd seen in movies: a combination of courteous and helpful, but formal. I wondered how much of her time was spent picking up and assisting young, wide-eyed foreign teachers like me.

As she spoke, I began stealing glances out of the window and was soon noticing a repeating pattern in the scenery: blocks of gray and off-white apartment buildings surrounded by rows of small indistinct shops one after another.

"Our university," Rose cut in after a moment's pause, directing my attention toward a big, gated compound to our left. Our car turned down a narrow side street opposite the university's gate, and Rose added, "I will show you our offices tomorrow. But first, your apartment.

"All employee housing," Rose said as we maneuvered around a few more tall gray apartment buildings. "And yours is here. Fifth floor. Top floor. No elevator. Is it okay?"

"Yes, fine," I said, looking up at the featureless building we were pulling up in front of. "It'll be good exercise for me."

She smiled. "Yes, I have read that you are very sporty."

I wondered, briefly, where she might have read this and then decided it was probably in some dossier that the agency had sent over. As we got out of the car, I quickly compiled a mental list of what non-selling points of mine the agency had likely tried to minimize:

1. Teaching Experience: None
2. Chinese Culture and Language Proficiency: None
3. Overseas Experience: None

But, yes, I had a college degree, knew English, and could climb multiple flights of stairs. For the time being, I could only hope that would be enough.

Again grabbing one of my duffle bags, Rose dismissed the driver and motioned for me to follow her inside the building. Taking the other bag, I did as instructed, and together we began climbing the ten narrow flights of concrete steps. I felt compelled to apologize to Rose for the size of my bags—the sheer mass of stuff that we were suffering under the weight of, and which I was now certain could have been reduced with more careful consideration on my part, seemed both comical and grotesque—but she waved it off.

"All the foreigner teachers bring as much," she said, looking remarkably unfazed, despite her slight frame and high heels.

I couldn't decide if this response made me feel better or worse.

Upon finally reaching the top floor, Rose took out a set of keys and unlocked one of two doors on the small landing.

"Now," she said as we set the bags inside, "I'm sure you are tired, but you will be more tired later with the jetlag, so I think it is best to leave your things and first go to eat. Then, I will take you to buy some grocery items for the morning, and we will return."

I nodded and, unable to decipher my stomach, looked out of the window at the waning daylight. I supposed this would be around dinnertime.

Back outside, we walked around the corner of the apartment blocks to where a little restaurant sat next to a small shop. Rose ordered us each a bowl of noodles, and after she had finished and I had eaten what my confused stomach would allow, we moved next door to the small store, where she picked up boxed milk, bread, jam, instant coffee, and a bag of oranges.

During the brief apartment tour, once we were back upstairs, I must have looked as out of it as I felt because Rose said, "You will sleep now. In the morning, I will call and come to fetch you from here. We will then go to hospital and to our office to complete your paperwork."

I wasn't sure why I needed to go to the hospital, but, too tired to keep the conversation going, I said only, "Okay, thanks."

"It doesn't matter," she said. "Warmly welcome." And with that, she left, and I was alone.

After preparing for bed, I brought out my journal, as had been my habit since my early teen years, and tried to capture the three exchanges that had punctuated my transition thus far: the blond woman, the businessman, and Rose. With my strange way of thinking that continually blurred the line between analysis and creativity, I had the sense that, though I could not now see it, someday, the connection between these apparently disparate experiences and conversations would become clear. Someday, somehow, they would become a story. At the moment, I had only to record it. Perhaps all young aspiring writers, such as I was, feel the same. Perhaps it is only later, in our real-life adult minds, that we begin to doubt, to wonder if this type of thinking only leaves us grasping at straws, trying to find or create significance where there was none. Perhaps the conversations, when seen in retrospect, would mean nothing; maybe they were random, talking simply for the sake of killing time, practicing English, fulfilling an obligation …

After jotting down these observations in my notebook, I made an additional note to remind myself to figure out the internet or calling card situation in the next day or two, as I had promised to let my folks know that I had arrived safely as soon as I found a way to. Then, switching off the light, I closed my eyes and, having just traded in everything I had known for an uncertainty, waited for physical exhaustion to quiet my restless thoughts.

CHAPTER TWO

~ *Taking On New Meaning* ~

I opened my eyes to dark and quiet. It took me a few moments to place myself, but once I did, I got up, unzipped one of my bags, and fished out my running shoes. At some point I hoped to get into a running routine here, but for the moment, I only wanted the shoes in order to retrieve the watch I had stuffed in one of the toes. There weren't any clocks in the apartment that I had seen. Pulling out the watch, I read *11:07 a.m.*, which at first did nothing to alleviate my disorientation. But, willing myself to focus on calculating the time difference, I did a quick bit of math. *Twelve plus fifteen, or was it sixteen?* I recalled reading that the time difference between the all-in-one-time-zone China and the U.S. west coast depended on if the U.S. was in daylight savings mode or not. *Spring forward, fall back … sixteen hours, then?* Doing the math and glancing out the window, I decided that three in the morning was probably right. Or close enough, anyway. The air definitely had that eerie small-hours feel to it.

Lying awake in darkness while awaiting morning didn't sound all that appealing, so instead, I headed down the short hallway to the bathroom to begin getting ready for the day. I checked the red light and dial on the water heater in the top corner of the bathroom, as Rose had instructed me the previous night during the tour, and then inspected the handheld shower nozzle and knobs. There was no shower curtain, but otherwise, it wasn't too dissimilar to anything back home. Rose had also pointed out that, though Chinese-style "squat toilets" were the norm, this bathroom had been fitted with a western toilet specifically for foreign teachers. In my brief research into life in China, I had seen pictures of these so-called squatty potties—holes over which one squats rather than sits—and though I was mentally prepared to adapt to them, I had to admit that I was happy enough not to have to on my first morning here.

After showering and dressing, I still had several hours until Rose was supposed to arrive, so I decided now was as good a time as any to start making myself at home. It was time to unpack and settle in.

My first thought was that the apartment was big. With two bedrooms, a living room, a bathroom, an office, a dining room, a kitchen, and a sunroom, it was by far more space than I had ever had to myself before, and it was certainly more than I had expected to have in China, a country famous for its large population and images of overcrowding. The living room was furnished with a brightly colored teal couch and matching loveseat, a coffee table, a TV, and an air-conditioning unit on the wall. There were a couple of remote controls, and I fiddled with each of them briefly, discovering that the TV had five channels, all in Chinese. The other remote, I determined, controlled the AC unit, but I couldn't make out the buttons with Chinese characters on them so instead scrawled a second line item on my reminder note, underneath the one about the internet situation, to ask for Rose's help in translating them. I recalled that the previous day had felt warm when I arrived at the airport, so I supposed air conditioning would come in handy. Living in a desert climate would be another first for me.

I spotted an office-style phone sitting on a small side table near the front door and noticed that there was a list of numbers lying beside it. Glancing over it, I guessed that this had been left by Rose since her mobile number was the first one listed. The rest of the numbers were identified as being for various offices at the university and emergency services. This was another thing that hadn't occurred to me: what to do in case of emergency. It was a strange feeling, realizing that calling 911, the response ingrained in me since childhood, was suddenly no longer an option. A bit unsettling, too, thinking that, even if I called one of these other emergency numbers, I would likely be unable to communicate. For now, though, I decided, there was nothing to be done about it except to hope that it wouldn't come up.

I turned my attention to the opposite side of the room and what had looked to me like a sunroom. It jutted out a few feet from the apartment building and was surrounded by three walls of ceiling-to-waist windows, which would let in plenty of light during the daytime, it seemed. But, able to think a bit more clearly now, I could see that if this had been intended as a sunroom, the design was fairly flawed: the space wasn't wide enough for so much as a chair, and with the windows stopping at belt level and cupboards going from floor to window, there'd be no view if a person were sitting down. Perplexed, I walked into the space and turned around. A crank hung on the inside wall, and, after hesitating a few seconds, I gave it a tentative turn. A gear-turning sound creaked above me. Looking up, I spotted two metal bars suspended by way of a pulley system bolted to the ceiling. The two bars began lowering with each turn of the crank, and my mind ran through their possible functions (exercise equipment? curtain rod? art hanging display?) until they stopped even with the bottom of the windows. Knowing this would obsessively occupy my mind until I discovered the purpose of such a contraption, I stepped closer to the window and looked out for answers. A vague early-dawn light showed a red clay track below, and I considered how the room might potentially serve as a spectator box. It was actually a great view: standing with elbows on top of the cupboard, from the height of the fifth floor, I could see, in addition to the sports field, a few fields in the distance, some construction cranes, and a number of other grayish apartment buildings like mine. I was almost distracted from my research until I turned to my left and saw the neighboring apartment's "sunroom," where clothes were hanging from their two metal bars. So, that was it then: a drying room.

From there, I moved to the kitchen, where I found a free-standing washing machine, mini fridge, propane stove, tiny countertop oven, and water cooler like those I'd only ever seen in office-based sitcoms and at the dentist's office. The dispenser had a red handle and a blue one, which was easy enough to figure out in order to make my instant coffee. The tiny oven took a little more time to work out for making toast, but with the aid of pictures in the provided instruction manual, I eventually did. Overall, I decided to count my first meal in my new apartment as a success, even if a simple one.

Returning to the drying room with another cup of coffee, I watched as the sun finally began to awaken the city and waited for Rose to come and take me out into it.

* * *

It was standard procedure, Rose assured me when we arrived at the hospital: all foreign residents were required to complete a physical examination along with the accompanying paperwork in order to work in China. The fact that I had just had to complete one less than two months ago in order to get the visa to come over in the first place seemed beside the point. She produced a large stack of papers from her attaché and went to speak with the receptionist. When she returned, she held yet another form, which she handed over to me.

"So many papers." It sounded like another phrase she was used to saying. "But this one is simple; just complete your personal details."

"Um ..."

She looked at me, expectantly, so I continued uncertainly, "I can't read it."

"Oh, yes, of course. My mistake."

Snatching the paper out of my hands, she set about writing the English translation beside each line.

When she finished, she handed it back to me, and in a matter of minutes, I was able to complete all but one line.

"I didn't know who to put for the emergency contact," I said, pointing to the item. "I would usually put my parents, but I don't think that would be of much help here."

"No, my mobile number is better. We have your parents' information at the school, but it is better if the hospital contacts me."

She glanced over the rest of the form and looked suddenly concerned. "Place of birth is Vancouver? You are not American?"

"No. I mean, yes. It's a different Vancouver," I said. "A smaller one. In Washington."

"Ah, yes, Washington," she said with obvious relief. "I know it."

"Not Washington, D.C., though," I said, guessing at what she might be thinking. "Washington State, on the west coast."

Eliciting only a look of uncertainty, I continued, "Have you heard of Seattle?"

"Seattle." She thought it over. "Seattle … Ah! *Xiyatu*. Yes, I know it."

"Okay." I took her word for it. "Well, Vancouver, Washington, is a few hours south of there. Just across the border from Oregon."

"I see. Vancouver, USA. Okay, no problem."

She gave a quick nod, stood, and walked back toward the receptionist.

While she was gone, I looked around the waiting room and saw nothing that registered as familiar. I tried not to stare at a baby who, while being held in the arms of its mother, had an IV sticking out of its forehead, but since everyone else was staring at me, it was difficult to avoid making eye contact. I settled on scanning the walls for something, anything, to fix on, but there were no posters to be found. The few posted signs that were hanging were text only, written exclusively in Chinese, so I just looked toward the reception desk like a kid in need of a picture book and waited for my guardian to come back and tell me what to do next. The voice of the blond-haired woman from the flight came suddenly to mind: *I can't speak a word of Chinese and probably wouldn't make it two steps in the country by myself.* And I began to wonder when, or if, I would fare much better.

* * *

"A new friend!"

Startled to hear what sounded like an Australian accent, I looked around to find two non-Chinese twenty-somethings standing in the room I had just entered: the Foreign Affairs Office, according to the sign on the door. Throwing up his arms, the Australian grinned big and added, "Welcome!"

"Shaun," said the girl standing beside him, "she's only just arrived. Don't freak her out too much." Smiling, she took a few steps over to me, stuck out her hand, and said with a clear Canadian vowel-rise, "Hi, I'm Kelly. This is Shaun. Sorry if we seem a bit eager—we just don't get a lot of other foreigners out here."

"The Chinese desert hasn't caught on with the backpacker crowd, yet," Shaun said as he walked over to shake my hand, as well. "But, hey, I'm feeling good about Yinchuan's rise in popularity. *Three* foreign teachers now … crikey."

"Okay," said an administrative-looking young Chinese man who had just walked in the door, "here are the class schedules. Ah …" He cut off as he noticed me. "I'm sorry, I did not know you had come. Warmly welcome you to Yinchuan Technical College."

He looked embarrassed but quickly produced a business card as Shaun introduced us.

"This is Beckham. He and Rose basically keep us alive. Don't know what we would have done the past two years without the help of the FAO." Then clapping Beckham on the shoulder, he added, "Absolute aces."

Beckham deflected these comments with a small wave of his hand. "No, no. I still have very much to learn."

He looked to be around our age, maybe just out of college himself, and, in crinkled khakis and a polo, was dressed less professionally than Rose, which only made him seem more of a peer.

"And I know you will be very eager for these," he continued, handing us each a few sheets of paper.

"Summer holiday really is over then, isn't it?" Shaun said as he accepted, then looked over, the papers.

He and Kelly compared documents for a few moments while I stood trying to make sense of mine.

"Not too bad," Kelly said before turning to me and asking, "How's yours look?"

Still scanning over the handout, I replied, "Uh, five classes, I guess, each meeting twice a week for two hours at a time. Does that sound right?"

"Yeah, that's what we all have." Kelly looked over my shoulder. "Nice, only one early class. And Friday afternoons off—not bad at all." Pointing to the remaining papers in my hand, she added, "And those are your class rosters. They'll tell you how many are in each class and the room number where each one meets."

"Between the three of us, we teach all the incoming freshmen," Shaun added, still looking down at his lists. "Beauty! I've got the Welding and Automotive majors again this year. They're always my favorites."

I flipped through the rosters for my assigned classes: Horticultural Technology, Radiology, Mechatronics, Pharmacology, and Nursing. The students' names were in Chinese characters as well as being phonetically transcribed, and the lists were long.

"So, there are about forty-something in each class?" I asked.

Beckham nodded. "Big incoming year."

I didn't see a calendar or any dates listed anywhere and was about to ask what day we were to start when Rose walked into the room. She had stayed downstairs when we first arrived, saying she needed to tend to something, and sent me on ahead.

"Sorry," she said, walking to a large desk at the far side of the room. "We have twenty Indian students who were meant to arrive today, but there has been a flight delay." Then looking at all of us, she added, "You have received your class schedules?"

"Yeah, they look good," Kelly answered for all of us. "And what day are we starting this year?"

"Ah." Rose looked down at the papers stacked in various piles across her desk. "This year, fall term begins very early." Shuffling a few papers around, she landed her finger on some notation and added, "The freshmen begin tomorrow."

***

"Schedules are always a bit of a surprise around here," Kelly said after the three of us had left the FAO and were heading to get lunch somewhere. "It can be a pain, especially when you have students knocking on your door on a Saturday morning, telling you, 'Teacher, we have class now,' instead of on the following Monday, as usual, because of the such-and-such festival or military exercises or whatever other random thing comes up. But," she paused briefly as she stepped behind Shaun and put her hands on his shoulders, "we do our best to roll with it, don't we?"

"Yeah, we have a good whinge now and then, but, for the most part, we get on," Shaun agreed, tilting his head back and putting his hands on hers.

I couldn't help but notice the stares and double takes we were getting from students as we made our way through the campus toward the front gate, and I figured now was as good of a time as any to point out that I didn't actually know how to teach, that I had never taught a class in my life, in fact, and that, since learning just five minutes previously that there wouldn't be any textbooks for our classes, which happened to start the next day, I had no real idea of where to start.

Shaun gave a wave to a group of students who giggled and waved back, then said, "No worries, you'll pick it up. Just remember that it's oral English, which means the only real trick is to get them talking. Most of them have been studying English, on paper, for years—heck, their grammar's probably better than mine—but they've never had to use it in conversation, so if anyone says anything to them, they usually just freeze up." He waved at another couple of students who beamed back at him. "So, that's our job: to help them stick a toe in the water."

I must not have looked very reassured because Kelly smiled and added, "You'll be fine. Most of them will just be excited for the chance to speak with a native English speaker—probably for the first time ever—so they just need a little push to get them going."

That evening, back in my apartment and discombobulated by the day's range of new logistics, I tried to comfort myself with the idea that surely this is how every pioneer felt at the start of a new adventure, even if the beginnings were somewhat more mundane than I might have imagined. True, I hadn't considered that I may need to relearn basic things like drying laundry and filling out standard medical forms or understanding a new way of thinking about time and schedules, and I certainly wouldn't have guessed that, in addition to hopefully learning some Chinese phrases and perspectives, I may pick up some Canadian and Australian ones, as well; and, sure, I imagined the things I'd be capturing in my notebook would be more like the scenes I'd read about in books of far-off lands: the bizarre foods, the exotic customs, the unchanged appearance of ancient empires ... But maybe this was what the modern-day explorer faced. For now, I just needed to figure out how to do what was to be my new job. I needed to figure out how to teach, and quickly.

CHAPTER THREE

~ *Winging It* ~

In the morning, I again awoke before the rest of the city, but this time I lay in bed until a sliver of dawn appeared through the curtains. Then I got up, showered, and ate the same breakfast as the day before: toast, coffee, and an orange. Having prepared a lesson plan the previous evening, I was, of course, ready much too early for my 8:00 a.m. class, so I sat at the kitchen table distractedly going over my notes while checking the time every few minutes. Finally, at seven thirty, when I could wait no longer, I packed up and set out. The previous day, after lunch, Kelly and Shaun had shown me where I'd be teaching, and I retraced the way now and found it without any difficulty. The classroom was empty, which was no surprise, as I was still twenty minutes early.

With nothing else to do, I stood at the lectern and looked

over my notes yet again until, around ten minutes before eight, the first of a small group of students trickled in. I had heard them chatting in the hall as they approached, but they, having apparently not expected to see me, seemed quite startled at my presence and fell immediately silent.

"Hi," I said, giving my friendliest smile.

I heard a few of them say, "Hello, teacher," in return, but most were looking down, and their responses, if any, were inaudible.

The next several students reacted similarly until, suddenly, one boy, at the instant he had seen me, turned and began shouting down the hall.

Turning to face me again, he said in English, "Just a moment, please, teacher," then stepped back into the hallway and stood there, continuing to shout. I could hear the sound of running footsteps, and soon the remaining students were filing in, panting. They offered breathless "Sorry, teacher" apologies and then, like the others, quickly found their seats.

The boy who had done the shouting stood at the front of the classroom, looking over the class, and then glanced at me again and said, "Okay, teacher. We are here. Please begin," before taking his own seat in the front row.

I stood as forty-four faces looked toward me in complete silence. Glancing at my watch, I saw that we were still five minutes early, but as everyone was clearly waiting for me to do or say something, there seemed little else to do but jump in. I looked down at my notes again and began shuffling the papers to get to the roster. Thinking I could start with roll call, à la *Ferris Bueller's Day Off*, I held the list of forty-four names, scanned the Chinese characters and their romanizations, then changed my mind and decided instead to start with something I knew how to pronounce.

Clearing my throat, I began. "Hello. My name is Anne

..." I turned and picked up a piece of chalk to write on the board, "... Henry. I will be your teacher this year."

An echo of *Anne Henry* bounced around the classroom.

"Today, I will introduce myself. Then, you will introduce yourselves."

A few students nodded. I couldn't tell if, as Shaun had suggested, the lack of response from the others was due to fear or to the fact that they simply hadn't understood what I'd said. At any rate, I had their attention, which seemed like a good start.

I glanced down again at my lesson plan on the lectern and began second-guessing what had seemed like a good idea when I had written it the previous night.

"But first," I continued, realizing there was no alternative now but to forge ahead, "I want to tell you a joke. Do you know what a joke is?" I wrote the word *joke* on the board.

This was met with a fair amount of chatter as students turned and spoke to one another in Mandarin, and then, supported by surrounding nods and sounds of affirmation, the boy in the front responded, "Yes, teacher, we know."

"Okay," I said, beginning to guess that the boy was some sort of class representative, "I will tell the joke, and you will try to guess the answer."

More nods.

I was suddenly reminded of a wedding I'd gone to earlier in the summer. When the best man had gotten up to speak, the room then felt very much like this now: thick with potential disaster.

"So the joke is: My arms are very tired. Do you know why?"

A few snippets of Mandarin sprung up again around the classroom. Then, once again, it was the boy in the front who spoke.

"Can you repeat, please?" he asked.

I repeated the question, this time pointing to my arms and feigning tiredness. Another ripple of chatter followed.

"Anyone can take a guess," I encouraged.

"Have you been ill?" one student asked suddenly.

"Have I been ill?" I repeated. I wrote *ill* on the board, paused for a moment, then struck a line through it.

"Good guess, but no," I said with a shake of my head.

"Maybe your luggage was very heavy?" another girl tentatively suggested.

I wrote *heavy luggage*, then crossed that out, as well.

"Good guess; my bags were very heavy. But … no, that's not the answer. Remember, the answer is supposed to be funny."

"From hitting your students when they are bad," one boy called out. A few students responded with shy laughter.

"Ah, hitting bad students," I repeated, again writing it out. "A very good idea." I smiled, then struck it out.

"But no," one student finished. A few more laughs floated around.

"Should I tell you the answer?" I asked.

"No. No, teacher. We will guess," the boy in the front said hurriedly.

After another few minutes of attempted answers, including one about carrying a baby and another involving the strain of learning to use chopsticks, the students finally allowed me to tell them.

"It's because I just flew all the way from America." I illustrated with a flapping motion.

The punch line wasn't exactly met with laughter, but after a few brief exchanges between students, I saw heads begin to nod, and then, much to my surprise, a round of applause arose.

I had intended to have the students spend the rest of the class practicing introductions and jokes in pairs and groups, but as I began to walk through the classroom in order to help where needed, I was immediately stopped by several students who asked if they could change their English names from the ones they had in high school.

I didn't see why not, so I said, "Sure, go ahead," and went to get the roster, thinking that now would be as good a chance as any to go through it and write the English names beside the Chinese ones in order to help me learn them.

But in the short walk to the front of the class, the news had already spread so that, when I turned back around, the room was a flurry of names and words and hands waving me over for assistance. Some wanted to find names with similar meanings to their own; many preferred names of celebrities—pop stars, NBA players, and actors, mostly; and then there were a few outliers: Yahoo!, Tank, Swallow, Superman, and Ta Ta. I told this latter group that those weren't really names, but they wanted to keep them anyway, so in the end I let them. I figured, hey, if you can't be creative in choosing your own foreign name, when can you be? I wrote them all down, and then, after practicing introductions with their new names, that was it. The two hours were over.

"Goodbye, teacher, see you next time," the students said one after another, heading out the door.

I waved, said goodbye and, when the last of them had left, let out a breath.

* * *

Over the next few weeks, I focused on all the necessities of settling in. I figured out how to access email and use a calling card for infrequent, but reassuring, overseas contact. I got a cell phone for in-country use and learned how to put minutes on it. I figured out the bus routes and where to go shopping for groceries. I learned how to say, "*Wo shi meiguoren; Wo shi yingyu laoshi*"—I'm an American; I'm an English teacher—and "*Duibuqi, wo ting bu dong*"—Sorry, I don't understand what you're saying. I learned numbers one through ten and how to pronounce the names of a few dishes to order in a restaurant. I could successfully direct a taxi back to my apartment, most of the time. I even got semi-used to the crowds and stares.

I was also surprised to find how quickly I began to view the elements of a new panorama as normal: bare-bottomed babies held out to pee over gutters and shrubbery; mule-pulled carts being led down a busy street; blue plastic tubs lining the sidewalk, filled with writhing eels for sale; bicycles teetering under the weight of gravity-defying Jenga-shaped stacks of crates or bags of vegetables or sofas ... sights that I found, at first, so odd-looking, but less than a month later hardly merited a second glance. I became a regular at the breakfast cart parked just outside the main gate to campus, stopping each morning on my way to class to get a *jianbing*: a combination of crepe, egg, and spices prepared fresh on the mobile griddle. And when I waved at the campus gate guard (who, with his slight frame and oversized uniform, looked to me like a boy playing soldier) and he waved back, always shyly but no longer requiring to see my ID, I felt that I had begun to be accepted as a somewhat normal sight, too.

Additionally, and importantly, I had established a running route. It took me a few days to work out where the various roads around me led and what combination of paths and streets would give me the distances I wanted, but once I had, I was setting out like I'd been running it for years: down the height of my apartment building, those ten flights of concrete steps, giving a few smiles and words to neighbors, out the door, past the old women gossiping in the courtyard and young men calling, "Hullo! *Waiguoren!*"—the Mandarin word for foreigner—then off into the street and crowds, maneuvering through track-suited students lining up for fried dough, placing their orders of disc-, ball- or stick-shaped, red-bean-filled or plain, sugar-glazed, sesame-rolled, chili-flaked, any four for a *kuai*, one *yuan* or *renminbi*—the currency of China, literally "the people's money," valued at an eighth of a dollar—each variety sitting in neatly-lined rows, sold and restocked by two young female workers dressed in white chef smocks with handkerchiefs around their heads, standing beside the vats of hot oil, tongs gripped firmly in hand, glancing up quickly at customers and down again as they plucked one dough item out after another.

Next, it was on to the line of wheelbarrow carts offering roasted peanuts, dried fruit, vegetables, and fresh meat … and then through the group of the fifty-gallon drums, split lengthwise down the middle, repurposed as grills, laid out with ears of corn, hot dogs, and sweet potatoes. Shouts of *Yi kuai! Yi kuai! Yi kuai!*, again a single *renminbi*, followed me in persistent enticement as I hustled past.

After navigating my way through these vendors and patrons, I would finally reach the end of the block, make a turn, and then, just like that, find myself surrounded by quiet. I continued down a dirt road with small plots of gardens along the side until I turned again to run along a small canal for a few miles, and, though the air was dry and most things were brown instead of green, it otherwise almost felt, for those forty-five minutes until I eventually hit another bustling paved road and circled back around to wind up again at my apartment, like being out on a country run back home. It was the closest I'd ever felt to being in two places at once. Conflicting … but exhilarating, too.

Of course, I had Kelly and Shaun to thank for much of my adaptation to life in Yinchuan, as well. They, with the humor and grace to avoid ever making me feel like a third wheel, showed me how to participate in the daily norms of a community, to move at an accelerated pace from the outside toward the in. Nearly every day, they showed me some place new: where to get the best deal on photocopies, where to buy CDs and DVDs without getting ripped off for being a foreigner, where to find the only English-playing movie theater in town (which was located in a back alley behind the main theater and, for some inexplicable reason, showed only B-grade horror films), and where to get the best of every kind of food. From spicy to sweet, traditional to modern, dumplings to hot pot, noodles to rice … my introduction to China took place over a host of textures and tastes.

In one such dinnertime conversation, one night in late September, the talk had turned to travel. It was a pleasant evening, still warm enough to be without a jacket, and the three of us had opted for eating at the open-air barbecue down in the city's Muslim quarter. We were there, at the edge of the plaza next to the city mosque, sitting on plastic stools alongside people of the Hui and Han ethnic groups which made up our city, with the smells of beef, lamb, and chicken kebabs commingling with the sparks that drifted up overhead from the grill, when Kelly brought up the fast-approaching National Day and asked where we wanted to go for it. Unsurprisingly, I had no idea to what she was referring.

"Right, I keep forgetting how new you are," she said when I confessed my ignorance. "October first is National Day. We all get a week off for it."

"Pretty grouse, right?" Shaun chirped.

By then, my Australian, like my Mandarin, had been making strides, so I translated quickly in my head: this was a good thing.

"A week off in October," he continued, "a week off in May, and six weeks off in January and February, between semesters, depending on the lunar calendar, for the winter holiday. If you use it right, you can really get some good traveling in."

The conversation paused momentarily as a Muslim woman wearing the traditional white cap of the Hui brought out our orders and refilled the pot of tea shared by everyone at our table.

"Of course," Shaun resumed after she had left, "pretty much everyone else in the country has the same idea about traveling during the holidays. But you know …" He shrugged, eyed the kebabs, then picked up a chicken skewer before finishing his thought, "… what better way to really experience the country than by shoving onto a train with a billion other people? Best way to get to know the culture, really, up close and personal."

"Uh huh," Kelly said in her customary role of steering the conversation back on track. "So, the question remains, where do we want to go? Anne," she said, turning to me, "you haven't been anywhere, yet—no offense."

"None taken," I said, laughing at the thought that, in this world, having not yet gone anywhere could be perceived as an insult.

"Where sounds good to you, then?" she continued. "What will inspire the next great piece of travel literature in our aspiring writer?"

I shrugged. "That's the beauty of it," I said. "You never know where you might find a story. Potential at every turn … especially when every turn is a new one."

Kelly smiled. "In other words, you're of no help." She took a sip of tea as she looked across at Shaun who had just bitten off a large chunk of meat from his third kebab. "Okay then, up to you, Shaun. Pick a direction."

With only the briefest hesitation, he raised a finger from his kebab-free hand and pointed downward.

"South," Kelly interpreted. "Well, we've always talked about going down to Yunnan Province to do some hiking. It's a bit of a journey, and we'll have to hustle to make it there and back in a week, but it's definitely doable."

Shaun nodded and swallowed. "*Hao da,*" he said—the Mandarin equivalent to "Sounds good."

They both looked over at me for consensus, so I contributed what I could, a clueless but willing thumbs-up. And, just like that, the future had been set in motion.

CHAPTER FOUR

~ *Learning The Way of the Open Road* ~

We left the Friday after classes. The details leading up to our departure had made little sense to me—Rose had had to help us get the train tickets because of something called *guanxi*, and we had had to decide our class of travel among the options of "hard or soft seat" or "hard or soft sleeper"—but it was most likely precisely for this reason that I felt no burden in the decision making. We would get tickets, or we wouldn't; we would enjoy our seat selection, or we wouldn't. There was little to consider when you understood nothing of the process.

Once we made it onto the train, though, I had a little more context in which to understand our arrangements. We had gone with the "hard sleeper" option, which apparently meant having a bunk on a wall in a set of three. It looked something like what I imagine beds on a military transport might be:

white-sheeted, bare-boned, hung with metallic supports, and stacked to within about two feet of the ceiling. About three feet over, another set of beds began. It wasn't a lot of space, but it was certainly efficient.

"Get comfortable," Kelly said when we found our allocated beds. Between the three of us, we had a bottom berth and two of the middle ones across from each other. Kelly and Shaun offered me the bottom, which had the most headroom.

"This is home for the next fifty hours," she added.

I mimicked Kelly in pulling a few items, including a book, out of my pack before sliding it underneath the bottom bunk.

"And count your lucky stars we're not traveling hard seat," Shaun said as he climbed up to the opposite middle bunk and began putting a few things in the netted pocket beside his pillow. "I went hard seat once—twenty-five hours between Beijing and Xining during a May holiday—and, no, never again. I had about half a seat, and it was so chock-a-block I could hardly budge. I had to literally squeeze my way past people, while trying not to step on anyone, just to make it down the aisle to the squatty, and when I finally did, there was some sheila sitting in the sink, asleep, holding a baby. Definitely not worth saving a few *kuai*."

Kelly and I took a seat on my bed after getting our things organized.

"So, what's the difference between the hard and soft sleepers and seats?" I asked as I watched the other passengers making similar arrangements in the areas around their beds. Bags of food and thermoses began piling up on the small tables underneath the windows. "Is it just like it sounds?"

Kelly set a bag of tangerines on our table, then threw one up to Shaun.

"Sort of," she said. "Basically, hard seats are the cheapest, but they can be brutal for anything over a couple of hours—

they're typically just wooden benches that people cram onto. Feels a bit like riding in a cattle car, if I'm honest. Soft seats are obviously more comfortable—more like an airplane seat, with a bit of a recline. Soft sleepers mean you get a separate compartment. Four beds to a section instead of six and with a door that closes."

"Quite a bit more expensive," Shaun added, peeling the tangerine. "And not all that much better. These are totally fine. Less elitist, and better for people-watching, besides."

Kelly motioned for me to scoot over, and Shaun jumped down to join us in sitting on the lower bunk. She held up a pack of cards as she said, "People-watching and these—all you need to survive a multiple-day train ride."

The train began to creep forward, and, looking out through the window at people making last-minute dashes from the platform onto the train, I suddenly remembered another question I had.

"So, why was it that Rose had to get these tickets for us, anyway?" I asked. "What's that *guanxi* thing you guys were talking about?"

"Ah, good old *guanxi*," Shaun said, taking the deck of cards out of its pack and flipping through them. "It means 'relationship' with kind of a dash of 'good feelings' thrown in. Put it this way: it's a whole lot easier getting train tickets during the holidays if you know somebody."

"And Rose does? Knows somebody at the train station?"

Kelly shrugged. "Or knows somebody who knows somebody. I mean, it could be an old school friend of hers who works there, or it could be her brother-in-law's uncle's cousin's son who's on the board of directors at the Department of Railroad Transportation or some such. Or she just has 'good feelings' with someone else who knows how to get tickets. The web can get pretty complicated." She received the deck of cards back from Shaun and began shuffling. "The main thing to remember is that China is a land of connections—a place where you literally need to make friends to get by."

"Hard to imagine you'd need more than us, I know," Shaun added, smiling as our train cleared the platform and began gaining speed. "But, in this case, it's true: the more, the merrier."

Just then, almost as if on cue, the old woman sitting on the bottom bed across from us tore open a packet of sunflower seeds and passed it around to the other people on her bed: an elderly man, and a younger woman with a baby. They had been watching us, I noticed, and soon the old woman held out the packet and offered it to us. Kelly and Shaun took some, then poured a little into my hand and thanked the woman in Mandarin. The old woman said something, and the old man followed it up with something else, and with that Kelly and Shaun became involved in conversation. In a matter of minutes, the other woman handed me her baby, who, like all babies I had seen in China, was wearing pants without any material over the crotch or bottom and was diaperless. I bounced the child tentatively and smiled. Not being able to understand what was being said, this was about as much as I could offer: my go-to enthusiasm and a mute smile. I did, however, take what Kelly and Shaun had said to heart. Despite being naturally drawn toward the conversations and characters that filled my mind and pages, here, it seemed, I would need to find a way to build up my *guanxi*, simply as a matter of survival.

Soon, someone had poured more sunflower seeds onto the book I had lying beside me, and, in an instant and much to everyone's amusement, the baby kicked the whole works onto the floor.

* * *

The majority of the evening was taken up with children—children who were brave enough to come see the *waiguoren* or, at least, whose parents were insistent enough that they should come try out their English. It worked out fine for me, since the kids didn't seem to mind my lack of understanding. In fact, they took great pleasure in teaching me simple words like those for colors and animals—*hongse*, red; *huise*, gray; dog says "*gou, gou*;" cat says "*mao*"—with peals of laughter following my attempted pronunciations.

At about nine o'clock, the children were called back to their respective parents, and the whole carriage began a sort of communal nighttime routine: heading towards one of the squatty toilets on either end of the car, taking turns at the sinks, washing faces, brushing teeth, then stripping down to undershirts and underwear and climbing into bed. I used the facilities myself once everyone else had finished, and I discovered that, while aboard a moving train, some things were easier said than done. But I managed, and my quads got a good workout in the process.

The lights went out just as I crawled into bed, and for a while I lay stretched out on my stomach, my head to the window and arms under my chin, watching as the country went by in darkness, a few lights dotting the distance. It was quiet, other than the rhythmic click-clack of the train, which, it had just occurred to me, must come from passing over the seams in the track. I had never thought about this before, but then again, why would I have? It seemed to me I had never learned or realized so many new things in such a short amount of time, not even in college, and it hardly seemed possible that I'd only been in China for just over a month. Promising myself that I'd get it all down in the journal tomorrow, I began going through a mental catalogue of the new words I'd learned from the day: *hongse*, *huise*, *gou*, *mao*—and the new concepts: *guanxi*, the need to make friends, the communal activity of sharing a bunk, the value of a deck of cards … but soon, with the gentle rocking, my thoughts tumbled together, and the train carried me into sleep.

* * *

Music, lights, and shouting woke me, and I pulled my watch out of the pocket beside the head of my bed: seven thirty on the dot. The shouting, I saw when the source reached our bay, was coming from a uniformed official. Everyone else was showing him their ticket, so I fished around in the pocket again and produced mine, too. After a quick glance, he moved on. Everything must have been in order.

"And you've still got your camera and wallet?" Shaun asked, hopping down off his bed.

I pulled back my covers and glanced over the two items. I had slept with them next to me, as Kelly and Shaun had advised.

"Yeah." I rubbed a hand over my face. "Slept pretty well, too. Successful first night."

"Aces," Shaun said. "Just a couple more days to go."

After a breakfast cart came by and we had had our steamed buns and instant coffee, we sat for a while, watching the passing scenery. It did certainly seem to be getting greener—not that that's saying much when you're coming from a desert—but still, it was a pleasant change.

We stayed inside our own thoughts for a while, reading and journaling, until Shaun abruptly broke the silence with, "Okay, five food items you miss most from back home. Go."

It had taken me a while after I first arrived to get used to these random talking points introduced by Shaun, but now I counted on them, brief moments to wallow in nostalgia and to come as close as we ever allowed ourselves to acknowledging homesickness.

"Right, okay." I jumped in and began counting off on my fingers, "My mom's blueberry pie, with berries picked straight from the garden … freshly caught Pacific salmon when my dad grills it up on the barbecue with lemon and garlic…gotta say pizza but, like, real pizza, Hawaiian, thin crust … then I guess it's a toss-up between a clam chowder bread bowl and chili with cornbread. Oh, and, of course, fish tacos and/or burritos; anything Mexican, really."

"Ahh, that one's the heartbreaker," Shaun said. "Mexican food. We're always on the hunt, but so far …"

Kelly reached up and began rubbing the back of his head. Turning to me, she said, "It's true. It's the one thing that has managed to elude us every year in China. Our white whale, of sorts." Then, in a mock whisper and a nod toward Shaun, she added, "I think it's slowly driving him mad."

"Captain Ahab and I like to think of it as *determination*," Shaun said, giving his best monomaniacal grin. Then, with a real smile, he added, "But I never lose hope in China—anything's possible here."

* * *

In this way, we traveled the length of the country, with hours and conversations blurring into each other, until, in the early evening of the second day, our train finally arrived in Kunming, the capital city of Yunnan Province. Cinching our packs tight around us, we made our way through the station, then, pushing past the mob of taxi drivers waiting outside, headed off on foot, guidebook in hand, in the direction of the bus station for one more overnight in transit. I felt as though I should have been exhausted, but instead, invigorated by something I couldn't quite put words to, I practically bounced down the sidewalk.

"How do you have that much energy?" Kelly asked, looking at me. "After two days and nights on a train, all I can think of is how nice it's going to be to pop a pill, pass out for this last overnight bus ride, and wake up there. Good lord, having a shower when we make it to our hostel in the morning … now that's what I'm excited about."

Shaun pushed his fingers through his tousled hair, then turned his nose into his sweat-stained armpit and took a whiff.

"I reckon it is about that time," he said. "Starting to feel a bit ripe. But, you know, organic is in. Maybe we should embrace it." He smiled as he threw an arm around Kelly.

"Yeah, well," she said, wrinkling up her nose and giving him a pat on the chest, "until you shower, have fun embracing it on your own." But then she gave him a kiss, anyway.

After buying our bus tickets, we had about an hour and a half to kill, so we went to a nearby restaurant and ordered a local specialty called "Crossing-the-Bridge Noodles." The name of the dish, according to our guidebook, was derived from a local legend in which a famous scholar's wife would carry the raw ingredients of his lunch—noodles, meat, and vegetables—across a bridge to the island where he studied, then cook them all in an oily boiling broth just before serving it to him, thereby avoiding soggy noodles. We agreed it was a good story and a good dinner besides.

This then sparked a conversation about how more food dishes should have origin stories behind them, and we continued it even after we boarded the bus, taking turns inventing our own legends behind popular foods. The banana split, Shaun claimed, had to do with a small-town doctor and a happy accident in the surgical room; the chocolate milkshake, according to Kelly, involved a skier in the Alps, a thermos full of milk, and a backpack full of chocolate; and the donut ring, per my imaginings, was the much-envied prize of jousting champions once upon a time. Shortly, though, the combination of the encroaching darkness outside together with the constant motion and our general fatigue caught up with us, and once again, we fell into unconscious silence. *The climbing ten-hour ride into the mountains offers views not to be missed*, I vaguely remembered the guidebook saying as I closed my eyes.

* * *

We awoke in the ancient city of Lijiang, and Kelly was right: after finding our hostel, a shower never felt so good. I was still fairly tired, having not gotten as good a night's sleep on the bus as I had during the train journey, so, as Kelly and Shaun headed out to begin exploring the city, I opted instead to take a book, along with my guidebook and journal, up to the hostel's rooftop beer garden. The sun was shining and, being just before lunch, it was the perfect temperature. Beautiful, temperate, fresh mountain air.

I had just reached the roof and was about to take a seat when I heard a male American voice from behind me ask, "Care to join?" Turning, I saw a guy in his mid-twenties, five-day stubble, with sun-bleached brown hair sticking out from under a Boston Red Sox cap and, most noticeably, brilliant sky-blue eyes—the kind that would have stood out anywhere, let alone in China. He was holding three beers, obviously having just come up from getting drinks downstairs, and motioned with his head behind him.

Looking over his shoulder, I saw a half dozen or so other backpackers arranged in a semicircle of metal chairs. One guy was holding a deck of cards.

I looked down at my stack of books a moment, then remembered my newly-received train-ride advice about living in China: *It's a place where you literally need to make friends to get by.*

"Sure," I said. "What are you playing?"

"Just a casual game of Hearts. No stakes involved. Unless you're terrible like me; then you might end up having to make the occasional drink run."

Somehow, I doubted that he was terrible. Hearts, I knew from Kelly and Shaun, was the game of choice among foreigners in China, and for some reason I got the impression that this guy had been around a while. Either that, or he was just one of those guys who always looked like he knew what he was doing. In any case, I followed him over to the group.

Sitting down in one of the empty chairs, I returned the nods and "heys" from everyone around the half circle. Counting Boston Blue Eyes and me, there were five guys, four girls.

"You have just arrived in Lijiang?" asked a guy who, by his accent, sounded German.

I nodded. "My friends and I just got in this morning."

"Night bus," a guy in a red maple leaf t-shirt said. "Brutal."

"Planning to hike Tiger Leaping Gorge?" one of the girls asked. I couldn't tell where she was from. Somewhere in Scandinavia, if I had to guess. The accent was subtle, but we looked as though we could have shared ancestors.

I nodded again. "Starting out tomorrow." Apparently, that was what people came here for.

"It's beautiful," said the German. "Incredible views."

"And it's doable in two days, I guess?" I asked. That's what we had planned for—staying two nights up there, one night back here in Lijiang, one night in Kunming, flying back to Yinchuan Saturday. A break-neck pace, we had called it.

"We took three days," the German answered, "but, yes,

you could easily do it in two. There are a few places to stay up there, so you can really go at whatever speed you like."

"Just don't arrive at the end too late in the day," Maple Leaf added as he finished dealing out the cards. "If you do, there won't be any rides back into town, and you'll have to wait until morning." After a moment, he played the Two of Clubs, then said, "If you make it by mid-afternoon, though, you should be fine."

"Alright, thanks," I said, both to Maple Leaf and the German. I wondered if Kelly and Shaun knew this already or if I needed to make a point of remembering it.

On the next trick, someone threw out the Seven of Spades, and Maple Leaf startled me by yelling, "Bring out the bitch!" Everyone else let out a groan and then, just as quickly, resumed conversation. The game, it seemed, was mostly incidental.

The talk throughout the hand stayed pretty much in the realm of where we were all from, where we had all been, and where we were all going. The three girls were, in fact, Scandinavian and were together—Swedes traveling throughout Asia on a gap year. The rest of the group, I learned, was composed of two German guys, an Argentinean who didn't say much, Maple Leaf who was actually from England, not Canada, but was quick to point out that from age sixteen had lived in Florida, and Boston Blue Eyes who was, indeed, from Boston, though he had been living in Kunming for the past three years. So, my hunch about him was right.

After playing another hand, the British Maple Leaf Floridian declared a drink break. I was still all right with mine, and Boston said he was good for now too, so as everybody else headed downstairs, the two of us stood and moved nearer to the edge of the roof overlooking the village. The sight—a seamless canopy of upturned tiled rooftops stretching out toward the mountains—reminded me of something out of a movie, and it apparently did for Boston, too, because, leaning out, he glanced down and said, "Kind of makes you want to jump down and run across the tops of them, doesn't it? Like some kind of Crouching Tiger ninja. Or, what's the other one? Hidden Dragon?"

I placed both hands firmly on the ledge and looked down briefly to gauge the distance to the cobblestone walkway below. "I think the only kind of ninja I want to be is the Mutant Turtle kind. Running around *under*ground sounds a bit more up my alley." Looking up, I took a couple of steps backward before adding, "Don't get me wrong, the views are amazing—just not a fan of heights."

"But maybe," he said, finally straightening up, "when you're running on rooftops, you don't notice the heights. Maybe it feels like flying."

"Maybe," I said. "But I still prefer to keep my feet on the ground."

He smiled and took a step away from the ledge to be even with me. "Well, it's probably for the best, anyway. The last thing we need is a bunch of tourists jumping around on eight-hundred-year-old roofs. I can only imagine what the UNESCO people would have to say. And, though I don't know about the underground options, I do know it's a great town to explore *on* the ground, by foot. Have you had much of a chance to? You mentioned that you just arrived."

I shook my head and pointed to the stack of books under my chair. "Still trying to narrow down the guidebook suggestions."

With a deliberate wrinkle of his nose, he said, "I don't know about those guidebooks. It feels like they take some of the personality out of travel. Some things are just more fun to figure out on your own, or, at least, to ask around about—you know, something a bit more interactive and not just out of a book."

"I am interacting," I said. "I'm asking the people who wrote this book what they recommend."

He smirked at that. "I mean, something a little less prescriptive. If you're just looking for something listed in the guide, you might miss a lot of other things."

"It just helps narrow down the options. A person has to start somewhere."

"Fine," he said. "What are you looking for?"

I laughed. "I don't know. That's why I have to look at the options first."

"Restaurants? Shops? Points of interest?"

I could see that he wasn't going to give up, and since I really didn't want him to, I threw out the first idea that popped into my mind. "Alright," I said. "My friends have been searching for a good Mexican place. Know of any?"

"Well, now that's interesting," he said. Pulling out his wallet, he slid out a business card and handed it to me. "See? You wouldn't get that kind of coincidence from a guidebook. You need to come to Kunming, though."

I looked down at the card and read aloud, "William Carmichael, Co-owner and Operator of The Foreign Burrito: Cantina & Grill—Kunming, Yunnan." Then, looking up again, I added, "Wow, what are the chances?"

He shrugged. "China's actually kind of a small world, when you start getting to know people. And you can call me Will."

"Will." I fished around in my bag, trying to fulfill my role in the Chinese etiquette of exchanging business cards, as I continued, "And how did you get into the Mexican food business?"

"It was kind of a series of happy and unhappy accidents.

But the short version is that a buddy of mine from college and I came over for a visit during the summer after graduation, and both of us being business majors and having a few connections, we just took the opportunity we were presented with. About a year of prep work and now two years running."

"Impressive. And … found it," I said triumphantly, tucking his business card into my wallet and handing him one of my own, using two hands as custom dictated. "My college gave me like five hundred of these, so I've got to use them when I can."

He smiled and said, "Nice to meet you," and now it was his turn to read off my card, "Anne Henry, English Teacher, Yinchuan Technical College."

Just then, the others started returning from downstairs, so we began making our way back over toward the chairs.

"Yinchuan," he said, turning my card over in his hands. "That's quite a ways up north, isn't it?"

"Just over fifty hours by train," I said as we took our seats. The stillness from moments earlier had now been entirely replaced by the rowdy banter of the group.

"Well, good thing China's a small world," he said as someone handed us both a drink.

* * *

We played Hearts for another half an hour or so until everyone started thinking about their plans for the rest of the day. I was waiting for Kelly and Shaun to come get me for lunch as we had planned, so I gave see-ya-laters to everyone as they got up and began leaving. I really thought I might see some of them later, maybe bump into those who were staying at this hostel or ones nearby over the next couple of days, but Will, I knew, would not be among them. He and his friends, whom he had to go find after their morning of souvenir shopping, would be heading to another town, he told me, about three hours south, later that afternoon.

"But, seriously, any time during the year when you want a break from the desert, or, you know, just need your Mexican food fix, I hope you do come back down. There'll be a burrito with your name on." He took a pen from his pocket and asked for his business card back. When I gave it to him, he turned it over and wrote, *Redeemable for one free burrito*, then signed his initials and handed it back to me. "There ya go, it's official now," he added. "You have to come back. And I promise you can stay on the ground."

"Promises, promises," I said. "But, yes, I promise I'll definitely try. After all, I can't pass up a good recommendation."

CHAPTER FIVE

~ *Changing Seasons* ~

When I think of it now, I remember the hike being as beautiful as promised and the rest of the trip being a success, but, more strongly, what sticks in my memory other than that rooftop conversation with Will is the feeling I had when the three of us first returned to Yinchuan. It was as though the week, the train journey, the interactions with fellow travelers had all set off something inside of me, and suddenly, as quickly as we had landed, I wanted to take off again, eager to follow up on all the future prospects of adventure and all the things still unseen. But there were still three months left in the semester—three months before the winter break and those six weeks of travel bursting with potential—so, I did my best to focus, for the time, on the smaller, daily experiences afforded by living in a foreign city, not just visiting one. I suppose it shows how little I've changed—my inclination is still to mentally jump ahead to the next big event circled on the calendar—but as I said at the beginning, maybe it's the things without obvious connection that, in reality, play the biggest role. Perhaps, as Virginia Woolf observed, the time between the acts is also worth examining.

So, upon my return, I began spending much of my time with students, over meals in the cafeteria, after class in their dorm rooms, making ramen in the small space between three sets of bunks, chatting about favorite bands, our families, the food back home, and whether or not I could use chopsticks. They wanted to know why I came to China and when I would marry. They came to my apartment to teach me how to make *jiaozi*, "the famous Chinese dumplings," and what method to use according to whose grandmother. And I took them, usually as a prize for some classroom competition, to one of the few Western-style cafés in the city, where I confirmed that, yes, pizza is a very popular food in America but, no, unlike in Yinchuan, corn and ketchup are not standard toppings.

We learned much from each other, and over a game of ping pong one Saturday, when I joked that "ping pong" was my middle name and then had to explain the joke, a group of them decided that it was time I had a Chinese name.

After conferring together for a few minutes in Mandarin, Ivy, one of the better English-speaking girls, declared, "We have chosen the name *Kang Jian*."

"*Kang Jian*," I repeated. "Very nice. What does it mean?"

A flurry of whipped-out electronic translators, which all students carried at that time, ensued until Ivy again spoke up. "It means Health Energy Bubble," she said, reading from her hand-held device.

"Health … Energy … Bubble," I repeated thoughtfully.

"Because you always do some sport and are very lively and

happy with us," Ivy explained.

"I am very honored," I said. "And I love it … I'm just not quite sure about the Bubble part." An image of a young John Travolta as *The Boy in the Plastic Bubble* popped into mind. "Do you mean like a ball? A ball of energy?" I shaped my hands into a sphere.

"No, teacher." She read again off her screen, "Happy, cheerful, and lively, like a bubble. It is English, teacher."

I smiled. "Yes, you're right, it is English. But sometimes even I don't understand it." Looking down at her small screen, I read for myself, *Bubble: happy, cheerful, and lively; like a bubble; a bubble personality.*

"Oh, bubbly," I said as it finally clicked. "A bubbly personality."

"Yes, teacher. Like a bubble."

The students smiled and looked relieved. The translators worked.

Having learned by now when to call it close enough when it came to nuances of language, I said simply, "Thank you. That is really a very thoughtful name."

"It doesn't matter, teacher," they all said quickly, obviously pleased.

* * *

Then, like someone had flipped a switch, it was winter. Or, at least, every outward sign suddenly indicated as much. I woke up one morning to find the radiator banging to life, and when I stepped outside, I saw everyone dressed in a big bulging winter coat and every doorway covered by a thick, green army blanket hanging down in front of it. Confusingly, the temperature felt exactly the same as the day before.

I didn't get a chance to ask anyone about it until the afternoon, when Kelly and I showed up to class and found our rooms empty.

"Oh, of course," Kelly said after a moment, "I totally forgot. Today's November fifteenth."

"So?" I asked.

"It's the first day of winter, as officially declared by the Chinese government. Every year, on November fifteenth, all of China north of the Huai River enters into winter mode, which means the heat gets turned on regardless of the actual temperature outside, and afternoon classes start thirty minutes later."

"Of course," I said. "Just when I was getting used to the schedule."

"You know what they say: *Jihua meiyou bianhua kuai*." Kelly held her hand out as though the empty classroom proved her point. "Plans can't keep up with changes. There's a reason that's a popular saying in China.

"Just be glad we don't live south of the river," she continued after we seated ourselves in two of my classroom's desks by the window. "They don't get heat down there at all. One of those leftover Cultural Revolution-era rules that does your head in if you try too hard to make sense of it."

"But why do people actually dress warmer? It's not a law, is it?" I asked. Honestly, for a child of the '80s, this idea seemed entirely possible. When it came to communism, who knew how far its reaches might go?

"Not a law, no," Kelly said cryptically. "But, I should warn you: if, from today until March fifteenth, when the heat goes off again and winter is officially declared over, you don't wear long johns and a big winter coat, you will undoubtedly suffer the chastisement of every grandmother in the city, a constant chorus of '*Duo chuan jian yifu!*'—Wear more clothes!—following you wherever you go." She mimicked this last part with a stern voice and a wagged, pointed finger.

A whole city full of Chinese grandmothers fretting over our well-being sounded kind of nice, actually, much nicer than the possibility of some inscrutable political party mandating our clothing requirements, and I told Kelly as much.

"Okay," she said, "but, personally, I'd rather take on the politicians."

* * *

When December arrived, however, we needed neither grandmothers nor politicians to tell us to wear long johns—the cold was dictator enough.

"Bloody hell! This might even be worse than the movie," Shaun said one evening when we all three stepped out of the theater and into what felt like a giant icy slap in the face. The night's offering had been an exceptionally bad slasher flick, but he was right. Fighting off a knife-wielding madman, in fact, almost seemed preferable at the moment.

As we all hastily fumbled with our coat buttons and zippers, Shaun nodded ahead and added, "But, hey, look."

Having prioritized the bundling on of hats, scarves, and gloves, it was a moment before Kelly and I dared lift our heads enough to follow the direction of his gaze, but when we did, we saw it. There, caught in the glow of the streetlight, danced a wild spiral of snowflakes. Unwrapping my arms from their tight hold across my chest, I slid off a newly-donned glove and stuck my hand out beyond the awning. A few tiny white specks landed and rested there briefly before disappearing.

They were right, I thought, as I watched more snowflakes land and melt, *I need to wear more clothes*. And with that, winter really had come to the desert.

* * *

Even after the snow arrived, though, I continued to run. I suppose there was something about going out and letting muscle memory take over that just gave me a sense of normalcy, even if it was only for an hour a day. It was nice knowing that, whatever changes China would throw at me and however out of place or in the dark I might feel, running more or less stayed the same. To avoid the coldest parts of the day and to take advantage of the best daylight, I went during *xiu xi*—the two hours in the middle of the day intended and used by most people for lunch and napping. Unlike when I had run in the mornings, now when I stepped outside, it was into the dead of quiet. Napping, I learned, was a serious business. With shops shuttered up and the bodies of sleeping workmen strewn along the roadside, slumped over steering wheels, huddled under carts, and tucked between bags of produce they had been peddling just minutes earlier, the scene looked almost apocalyptic. But it was peaceful, too. The city was sleeping, and for a little window of time, I passed through unnoticed.

And this is how the remainder of the semester went. For the final stretch, the FAO threw a joint Christmas-*Dongzhi* (aka winter solstice) party, where we sang Christmas carols and consumed rice-ball soup and *jiaozi* dumplings, which, we were told, because of their anatomical resemblance, would keep our ears from getting cold. We were given a winter holiday travel bonus in the same way we got our monthly salaries, in an envelope stuffed with cash, and were wished an early happy New Year.

Then, when New Year's Eve rolled around, it was like nothing I had ever heard before—topping even the most extreme of Fourth of July celebrations. I had been told that the "western calendar" New Year was actually quite a subdued affair compared to the Chinese date, which, based on the lunar calendar, was still weeks away, but the night seemed anything but subdued to me. Alight with firecrackers, the city snapped, sizzled, and banged from every corner. One could see them everywhere: long, red fuse-lit strips dangling from windows, thrown into streets, bouncing among cars, sending pedestrians scattering off sidewalks, and all night long the air filled with their steady stream of pop, pop, pop. In the morning, the vast debris of red paper and lingering scorched gunpowder marks gave the streets a sort of post-war-zone look. But no one seemed to mind. If it had been a war, it appeared that we were the victors, for we had made it into another year.

Mid-term exams proved to be a somewhat dreadful affair, both for my students and for myself—dreadful for them because the oral portion had to be done one-on-one with me, and regardless of how "lively and happy" I was with them, I was still a native English speaker, which flooded them with nerves; and dreadful for me because one-on-one examinations with three hundred students was a logistical nightmare, taking a week plus the weekend to complete—but, in the end, we made it through. And when my last student stood and, with visibile relief, said "see you next term" before rushing out the door, I couldn't say that I blamed him. After almost five months in these rooms, with very little break, it was now as though we all collectively let out one giant exhale, more than ready for the six-week winter holiday ahead.

CHAPTER SIX

~ *Going Oft Awry* ~

"Expats in China are like birds," Kelly had explained. "We all flock south for the winter."

And the three of us were to be no different, traveling south, at first separately—I again down the country by train, and Kelly and Shaun by air to visit a friend in India. Then, after two weeks, we would meet up in Bangkok and spend the remaining month island- and beach-hopping around Thailand. Buoyed by the tales of backpackers and adventurers that once filled my bookshelf—despite now being relegated to the boxes in my parents' basement back in the U.S.—and motivated by some deep, uncharted desire for inspiration, I charged forward without hesitation. Sure, I was to be on my own for the first time, but with one semester of living in China under my belt and a guidebook and journal in hand, I felt more than ready.

This time, I stopped at whatever places piqued my interest—the Terracotta Warriors in Xi'an, the panda breeding center in Chengdu, a giant waterfall in some valley the name of which I couldn't pronounce but, surprisingly, was able to find with the help of my book and the patience of train and bus station ticket agents—and I enjoyed being able to move at a pace entirely of my own. I noted down my observations whenever I had a chance—on trains, in hostels, over meals at cafés—and my thoughts wandered, sparked by the vast and varied cultures and lives I saw playing out before me in whichever setting I found myself. I could, I felt, quite happily carry on like this indefinitely and wondered if, and how, traveling could be a calling.

My thoughts continued in this vein, brimming with endless possibility and the growing belief that this was the start of something, as I pulled into my final destination in the country—once again, in the southern province of Yunnan, in the city of Kunming. Ostensibly and sensibly, I had chosen Kunming because of its large international airport. From here, it was only one short, cheap flight to Bangkok, my ticket to meet up with Kelly and Shaun in a few days having already been secured. Of course, though, the ulterior motive was obvious, if only to myself: it was the only city in China in which I had a standing invitation to visit. Plus, I had promised I'd try.

After checking in to my hostel and putting my bags down, I wasted no time in heading out toward the only place I knew. I took the card out of my wallet and flipped it over as I walked. *Redeemable for one free burrito* still lay scrawled across the top, and underneath that, a map of the city with a red star promised to guide the way.

The restaurant was only a few blocks from where I was staying, and en route I could tell that I had entered into a sort of student/backpacker area of the city, passing several bars, a handful of coffee shops, an internet café, two used bookstores, and a music/DVD shop, all within a few minutes' span. Then, suddenly, the hand-painted yellow letters of The Foreign Burrito sign hung above me. I put the card in my pocket and walked in.

The restaurant was quiet, but within seconds a Chinese girl, maybe around my age, appeared from the kitchen and asked in clipped but confident English if I wanted a seat. I nodded and followed her to a table, and when she asked what I would like to drink, I instinctually ordered tea. But then, as she turned to go, I caught myself and changed it to a Tsingtao. I wasn't yet at a place in my cultural fluidity that tea and Mexican food sounded, in any way, right together.

After the girl had come back with my drink and left again after taking my food order, I sat alone in an otherwise empty restaurant, waiting. Instead of pulling out my book or journal as I had for every other meal on this trip, I began fidgeting with my beer and thinking. Thinking ... which almost instantly turned into doubting. Yes, I had been invited, but isn't that just good marketing? I had been invited to the restaurant, and I had come. I could eat, then leave and try to think nothing more of it. I could approach my time in this city as I had any other unknown Chinese city—explore whatever the guidebook suggested, then move on to the next place. It didn't have to mean anything. Random encounters could be just that: simply unconnected moments along the way. Or, if they did serve a purpose, maybe this was it, to draw us in one direction, briefly, until the next interaction drew us elsewhere.

Needing to clear my head and wanting to try to recapture my earlier gusto, I got up and walked over to the metal spiral staircase, leading to what looked to be a loft. Making the short climb up, I discovered that I was, in fact, not alone.

A small group of what seemed to be college-aged students sat lounging shoeless on a set of couches and pillows. They gave the usual "Hullo" greeting, but it was more subdued than the usual shouts I got up north. It was nice, actually, for my foreignness to not be made such a big deal out of for a change, and I gave a little wave in reply before heading back downstairs.

Back at my table, I waited a few more minutes for the food to arrive, and when it did, it smelled of spices and heat. I ate slowly, and just as I was finishing, a Caucasian guy emerged from the kitchen. It wasn't Will, but I remembered there being mention of a partner and figured this must be him. We chatted briefly, the usual where-you-from, where-you-going type of stuff, and he seemed a nice enough guy. But I left it at that, deciding not to mention anything about my rooftop conversation with Will or the free burrito business card. It was just one conversation, after all; down here, they probably had many just like it. And who knew, maybe I'd come back.

"Enjoy Kunming," the guy said after I finished paying.

"Thanks," I said, turning toward the door.

The girl who had been standing at the bar, doing some sort of tallying over a notebook, gave a belated "See you," and as I turned to give a farewell nod, I pushed on the door and took a step—a step directly into someone coming in.

"Sorry," we both said simultaneously.

I looked up and saw a blue Boston Red Sox cap.

"Will. Hi," I said. Then, "It's Anne. We met in Lijiang."

His expression changed into a smile as he said, "Anne. Of course. October holiday. You were the one who was going to jump down and run across the rooftops, ninja-style."

"I think that was your idea," I said.

"Oh, that's right. I was the crouching tiger; you were the turtle, as I recall."

"Good memory," I said, feeling both relief and, honestly, a boost of confidence.

"Yeah, well, it's not every day that you almost get coerced into defying UNESCO."

"Again, your idea," I said.

"Hey, you have your version; I have mine." He looked toward the door and then back at me again. "But are you leaving? Did you eat already?"

"I just finished. I came almost directly from the train station. I mean, I'd been dreaming of this Mexican food for three months, after all, ever since you mentioned it." Then, I added quickly, "And, yes, it was as good as promised. Thank you."

"Well, at least, tell me that Roger and Mei hooked you up with a free burrito or something."

Reading the look on my face, then glancing at the guidebook in my hand, he shook his head and said, "Wait, wait, hold on. I can't, in good conscience, have you come all the way to Kunming, pay for a burrito, and then leave to explore the city based only on your guidebook. It truly goes against everything I believe in." He paused a moment, then continued, "How about you come back this evening, if you're free? I have to help prep the kitchen now for the dinner crowd, but there should be a good group tonight, being Friday, and you can get a feel for the real vibe of the city. How long are you here for?"

"Three days," I said.

"Perfect. Come back tonight, and we'll get you sorted. Sound like a plan?"

"Okay," I said. But you know what they say about plans.

* * *

It was still early, not yet two o'clock, and with the sun shining and my energy level heightened, I considered how best to put it to use. It felt good being out and about, moving under my own power instead of being driven by the constant momentum of the train, and that is undoubtedly what inspired my next idea. I returned to the hostel and got ready for a run.

I set out, at first passing by the standard string of businesses—post office, mobile phone vendor, catch-all convenience mart, photocopy shop, several *jiaozi* restaurants with their bamboo steamer baskets sitting outside the door—but soon, I began to notice the differences between Yinchuan and here. I saw taller, sleeker buildings, skyscrapers even, and not a mosque spire or dome in sight. I came across more businesses that I was familiar with from home: after four city blocks, I stopped counting at two Starbucks, two Dairy Queens, and three McDonalds. And there was a river that cut right through the city, which I followed for a while, sticking to the manicured foot and bike path provided alongside. Splashes of color from the trees, flowers, and grass, in addition to the waves of floral scents and the sensation of breathing dense, fresh air, removed any further trace of confusion between the two places: I was definitely no longer in the dryness of the desert.

I ran past a zoo and into a park and saw a sign directing visitors straight ahead with an arrow and the words "Green Lake" written in various languages. Then, in the next minute, I saw that it was more than just a name. The lake was, in fact, green, but beautifully so, dotted with lily pads and encircled by weeping willows along its shore. It was a big park, with benches and pagodas—and old people. Lots of old people. Everywhere I looked, I saw them playing mahjong, absorbed in tai chi, holding hands with what, I had recently realized, would likely be the only grandchild they would ever have—

the result of two generations born under a one-child policy. Up ahead, I saw a group of these elderly men and women dancing, ballroom-style, in an open courtyard. They were accompanied by the two-stringed *erhu*—the Chinese violin, as my students called it—and I watched as they glided gracefully in step, seemingly as weightless as the reedy bittersweet notes floating out over the water.

After circling the expanse of the lake, I decided I had gone far enough and so turned back out to a main road heading in the direction of the hostel. Even from the sidewalk, I could tell that the afternoon rush was kicking in. There was movement from every direction with cars, people, and bikes, all weaving in and out of each other's paths in a way I could make no sense of. I got penned in behind a crowd, and then, as a gap opened, I darted forward, picking up speed to pass through before the opportunity closed. From an alley up ahead, a delivery truck lurched forward, and, seeing it, I came to a quick halt. But the same couldn't be said of someone or something coming up from behind me. They had not reacted in time, and I was blindsided, hard. I found myself on the ground, tangled up with something metallic, and with a stabbing pain cutting through my left leg, I kicked out with my right. The metal thing shifted, so I kicked and pushed again and freed myself. Or maybe others had done it for me. I saw feet and legs gathering all around me, and I could only hope they meant me no harm. My head pounded amid the blare of car horns, and, suddenly drained of strength, I was able to do nothing but close my eyes and lie still, leaving myself in the hands of the crowd.

* * *

Within what may have been a minute, I was lifted and laid in the back of a car. I opened my eyes, briefly—it was not an ambulance, I could see that much. Was it a taxi? I heard shouting—the word for money—and I hoped it was not directed at me because I had nothing on me—no money, no phone, no ID. I had only the running clothes I was wearing.

And then we were stopped, and with my arms draped across the shoulders of a stranger on either side, I was half walked, half carried inside. I kept my eyes open now and could see that it was a hospital.

"Thank you," I said, as I was set down across a row of connected plastic chairs. "*Xie xie.*"

My legs were covered in blood, and the chairs underneath me were soon smeared, too.

"Sorry," I said, but there didn't seem to be anyone left nearby to hear. Whoever had brought me was gone, and in my hand I held a wad of crumpled-up cash.

A nurse soon arrived, and I held the money out toward her, not knowing what else to do. But she shook her head and pushed a piece of paper and a pen toward me. Pointing at the paper, she said something I didn't understand.

"I'm sorry, I don't understand," I said in English. And then the Mandarin phrase came back to me, and I tried again with a shake of my head: "*Wo ting bu dong.*" It felt suddenly important that I was able communicate this, at the very least—that I couldn't understand any of it and that I was truly sorry for it. "*Duibuqi,*" I added by way of apology.

She looked concerned but nodded patiently. "*Mei guanxi,*" she said—It doesn't matter.

I didn't see how that could be true. It seemed like it very much did matter. But I supposed it was automatic. Nothing ever mattered in China, even when it so clearly did.

She stood over me and inspected the cloth that someone

had wrapped around my left knee. She nodded again, and once more pointed at the form.

"*Mingzi*," she said carefully, her finger resting on the first line. "*Diahua haoma*," she added, moving her finger down a row.

My head was still pounding, but I tried my best to concentrate. Looking down at the Chinese characters on the paper, I suddenly heard Rose's voice saying, *Vancouver, USA. Okay, no problem.* I remembered then—they wanted a name, date and place of birth … and emergency contact. Without my phone, though, I didn't have any numbers to give. Then, as soon as I thought it, I realized I was wrong. I did have a number. I reached into the small zippered pocket of my shorts and pulled out Will's business card. At the last minute before heading out, I had tucked it in there, thinking that if I got lost, I could reference the map on the back. I handed the card over to the nurse.

"*Duibuqi*," I said again, noticing that my hand, too, was covered in blood.

But she seemed not to hear, looking, instead, intently at the card. I pointed to the name, which was also written in Chinese characters, and the number below it, and she gave another nod and rushed off. Immediately another young woman appeared in front of me with a wheelchair. She helped me into it, and I again could do nothing as she pushed me across the waiting room and toward the set of double doors.

* * *

"Anne."

My eyes were closed, and I wondered for a moment if I were asleep.

"Anne," the voice said again.

With my eyes still closed, I placed myself in the context of my surroundings—the hospital room, the examination table on which I was lying—then I opened my eyes to see Will standing beside me.

"Hey, turtle girl," he said. He looked as though he were trying to force a smile.

I began to prop myself up on an elbow but, with protests from every muscle in my upper body, thought better of it and immediately lay back down.

Will said something in Mandarin to someone at the far end of the room, and I turned my head, a movement which thankfully didn't scream at me too badly, to see the nurse who had helped me into the wheelchair earlier. She was preparing a syringe and a tray of various medical supplies, and offered a brief reply while continuing her work. Just then, a man walked in who, from his white coat, I guessed was the doctor, and they all three spoke for a minute or two together. I was relieved at not having to participate.

"Okay," Will said as he and the doctor returned to stand beside me at the examination table. "The doc's going to look you over, and you just tell him what hurts and what doesn't."

I nodded.

The doctor took my right arm and bent it.

I shook my head. "No, nothing," I said.

The other arm had a few scrapes and bruises, but it also bent at the elbow without any particular pain.

"Ahh," I winced as he pushed a spot on my ribcage. "Yes, there."

He said something to the nurse who scribbled it down on a piece of paper.

"Probably a couple of fractured ribs, he thinks," Will told me.

The doctor did some more prodding and bending and

spent a good deal of time inspecting my injured leg. He then shone a light in my eyes and asked me to track his finger as he moved it back and forth. When he had finished, he and Will stepped to the side of the room, and the nurse came over with some gauze and antiseptic and began cleaning the bloody mess around my knee.

"Well, good news and bad news," Will said, turning back to me as the doctor headed out of the room. "Bad news is, in addition to the ribs, it seems you have a concussion."

I drew a sharp breath as the nurse dabbed at the cut.

Will grimaced empathetically, then continued, "And it looks like you'll need about thirty stitches in that gash."

Stitches and a concussion—the same combination that I had gotten in a snowboarding accident a few years ago. Ski patrol had come and strapped me to a sled-type basket to haul me down the mountain. The blood from my head had left a big red blotch in the snow.

"You'll have to come back in a couple of days for a follow-up," Will was saying, "but after the stitches, they'll discharge you today."

"Okay," I said, still remembering the red snow. "And the good news?"

"That is the good news: you don't have to stay here overnight. Unfortunately, because of the concussion, you have to have someone check on you every couple of hours throughout the night, but I told him that I can help with that. I've got a spare room at my place, and you'll definitely be more comfortable there than here. That sound alright?"

"I've got my stuff at the hostel," I said, more as a statement than any real point of contention.

"That's no problem. We'll swing by and pick it up after we leave here."

"Okay," I said, deciding with what little clarity I could

muster that this probably made more sense than asking some random backpacker in the hostel to look in on me every few hours. On the mountain, they had stitched me up right in the ski lodge, and then I went back out and rejoined my friends to finish the rest of the day on the slopes. I was uncomfortable and in pain, but it was better than sitting alone in the lodge.

Something pinched my leg, and I looked down to see the nurse injecting the needle directly into the cut. I reflexively clenched my jaw and fists.

"Best not to watch," Will advised. "And if it's any consolation, I had a trip to the ER during my first few months in China, too. Of course, I'm sure this wasn't your fault, and mine most definitely was—sliced my hand open while cutting an avocado. It was a real bummer, too, 'cause avocados are hard to come by over here. Talk about some expensive guacamole."

He may just have been trying to divert my attention from the stitching, but his story reminded me of something from earlier.

"I was dropped off with a wad of cash," I told him, trying to look down around the table as much as my limited mobility allowed. "I don't know what happened to it."

Will spoke with the nurse who continued working on my knee.

"They took it at reception," he said after a brief exchange. "And it was enough to cover everything, so no problem. You might even get a little back."

"Oh, okay," I said.

Will smiled. "It's not really as shady as it sounds. Probably whoever's fault it was, or at least whoever's fault the crowd decided it was, just didn't want any trouble. And an accident involving a foreigner is always trouble—draws too much attention. So they just dropped you off with the money. Saves getting the police involved and doing all the paperwork."

"Okay," I said again, closing my eyes and putting my hands behind my head to lean back against. Suddenly, I began to see the appeal of that Chinese default response I had heard so often. Whether from exhaustion or due to a deeper resignation to a system so out of my control and understanding, it seemed the only answer that could grant some peace of mind, even if only for a moment. "*Mei guanxi*," I added. It just didn't matter.

* * *

When the nurse was finished, I looked down to see, instead of a gaping wound, a clean white bandage covering my knee.

"Came to thirty-six stitches," Will said as the nurse set the tools on the counter and disappeared for a moment. The bright, sanitized patch on the knee clashed grotesquely with the blood-stained shorts and shirt I was still wearing.

The nurse returned with a wheelchair, and Will, who was gingerly trying to fit a running shoe, also blood-spotted, back on my good foot, seemed to read my mind. "Don't worry, we'll stop by the pharmacy and get you some crutches."

In the taxi, I was helped into a position similar to how I arrived at the hospital: half lying, half sitting across the back seat. Strange to think that had only been a couple of hours previous. I wondered, briefly, if someone had put a towel down on the backseat when they had driven me here. It seemed likely they had not, which meant that the driver, whoever it was, had probably had to spend some time cleaning blood out of their car, as though it were a crime scene in need of wiping down. I guess we were both coming away with a story.

Will sat in the front, directing the driver to the hostel,

which I only remembered the name of, but Will said he knew. We were soon there, and in a matter of minutes after jumping out of the taxi, Will returned with my bag.

"No problem," he said after putting it in the trunk and taking his seat again. "They wish you a speedy recovery."

I tried to recall something specific about the place but couldn't really. I had spent less than half an hour there in total and had left virtually no trace of my visit other than an empty unslept-in bunk-room bed.

At the pharmacy, Will hopped out again and came back with the pair of promised crutches, as well as some bandages and drugs.

"All set," he said as though he did this every day, as though being called to the ER to help out a person he barely knew and then bringing them home to his apartment to let them stay in his spare room while they recovered from a concussion was just par for the course of living in China. And maybe, for him, it was. Maybe this wasn't the first time it had happened; him helping out some befuddled misfortunate backpacker who might have stumbled into his restaurant seemed entirely plausible. And maybe he thought the same about me; maybe showing up at a hospital, bloodied with no ID, holding only a wad of cash and a single business card wasn't an anomaly in my life, either, for all he knew. Other than what little we'd gleaned from a single conversation over three months ago, what did we really know about each other?

When we arrived at the apartment, Will helped me to the guest room, and after making sure I had everything I needed, he guessed, correctly, that I must be tired.

"Unfortunately," he said, "per doctor's orders, I do have to check on you, briefly, every few hours due to the concussion thing—I guess to make sure you're still breathing and, you know, haven't choked on your own vomit—but other than that, you can sleep as long as you like. Or as long as you need, I should say. I'm sure sleeping all day isn't exactly what you had planned for your travel adventures. Sorry about that."

"Well, I'm sure this isn't the itinerary you had planned for your day, either. I know you're busy at the restaurant ..." I trailed off, suddenly feeling an overwhelming need to lie down, to crawl into bed, to stop thinking, to stop moving, and to just be done, with everything. I knew more decisions would need to be made, but whatever they were, they could wait until morning.

* * *

"Sorry about last night," Will said when I had clumsily shuffled my way out of my room and into the kitchen by way of unpracticed crutch steps. "Hopefully you got some decent rest in between the are-you-still-alive checks. How do you feel?" He got up from the table and pulled out a couple of chairs, motioning for me to take a seat.

Every part of my body protested movement. I felt like I'd been through one of those industrial compactors, like the kind that crush scrapped cars into pancakes at the junkyard. My head threatened to explode. But, instead, I said, "I don't actually remember you waking me at all. But thanks. I hope I didn't give you too hard a time."

"Mostly, you just ignored me and kept breathing, which was good." He poured a mug of coffee from a French press and handed it to me. "Eggs and potatoes coming up if you're hungry," he said, sliding over the milk and sugar. A laptop sat by his spot at the table, and I suspected that he had been up for some time and had already eaten.

"Thanks, but don't go to any trouble," I said. "Or any more trouble than you already have." I tried to recall when last I had eaten … then remembered it was just yesterday, lunch at his restaurant.

"No trouble." He turned on the stove then walked to the refrigerator and pulled out some items. "I like to think that what I lack in medical expertise I make up for in cooking. Like my mom always said, 'With the right meal, we'll have you as good as new in no time.'"

"Speaking of which," I said, stirring my coffee and trying not to wince as I did so, "I really appreciate you having me here, but I'm sure you have a life to get back to. After breakfast, I can probably head back to the hostel and manage on my own for a couple of days until heading out." Managing on my own in my current state didn't sound the least bit appealing, but at this point, it didn't seem right that two people's days should be entirely derailed.

"We're actually plenty well-staffed at the restaurant with student help on the weekends, so there's no need to rush on my account." He had briefly turned from his place at the stove to address me, then, spatula in hand, turned back to resume his work over the skillet. "Anyway, the doc specifically said for you to take it as easy as possible for the next few days, and I would guess that you'll get more rest at this apartment than at a hostel. Your follow-up is on Monday, so you're more than welcome to just hang tight until then."

"Monday," I said. I thought for a moment, remembering that before all this I had planned to pack as much as possible into this weekend. "My flight to Bangkok is Monday afternoon."

Will brought the skillet over and tipped a pile of scrambled eggs and potatoes onto my plate and then a few onto his own.

"Yeah," he said, taking a seat, "I can help you figure that out."

I didn't know what it was exactly—whether it was what

he said or the way he said it, or if it was just that same confidence that Kelly and Shaun always seemed to exude, that you-learn-to-roll-with-it flexibility that perhaps came with years of experience as a foreigner living in China—but whatever it was, it helped put me at ease. With Will, it just seemed like things would always work out.

* * *

In the taxi en route back to the hospital on Monday morning, Will once again sat up front, chatting with the driver, while I sat taking up the back. This time, though, I felt much more aware, both of the situation and of just how lucky I'd been. I knew I was lucky to not have been injured worse than I was and doubly lucky to have had Will's card on me at the time of the accident, to have been taken care of, fed and allowed to rest and read, but also to be taken in by someone who, aside from being genuinely interesting and easy to be around, knew and cared whether or not I woke up in the morning and was still alive and able to move. It was, all things considered, maybe even one of the more relaxing weekends I had had since coming to China, with nothing I needed to do and nowhere I needed to be. But, lucky or not, I still couldn't help feeling disappointed, because I knew, too, that realistically I would not be going to Thailand. After the morning's appointment, I knew I would have to change my ticket and fly back up to Yinchuan. I had gotten in touch with Kelly and Shaun the previous evening and had told them as much, and now it was only a matter of hearing the doctor confirm it.

"He says it'll be about six weeks before you have full mobility again, because of how deep it was, I guess," Will told me as the doctor made his examination. The scan apparently showed no other major damage. "At least give it a month until you try running again."

The doctor bent my good leg and pointed to the skin stretched over the kneecap, then turned and pointed to the deep purple gash slicing across the straightened knee of the other.

"He's showing you what not to do. Try not to bend it. Or, at least, bend it as little as possible." Will said something to the doctor before continuing, "Stay on crutches for another week, and keep it as clean and dry as you can. Don't go swimming, and keep it out of the sun. I guess because the new skin would burn easily."

"So, as expected, Thailand's out," I said. "How about flying? When does he think I can head back up to Yinchuan?"

Will spoke with the doctor again. As he did, I noticed that the other patients in the non-private room seemed to be profoundly interested in my situation and were offering me their sympathy, encouragement, or advice—I couldn't tell which. But even though I couldn't understand their words, I was oddly comforted by their concern. It struck me that the West must feel like an awfully lonely place for people used to this communal input.

"Yeah, sorry," Will said, turning back to me. "He thinks Thailand would be a bad idea. As for flying back up to Yinchuan, he says if you really have to, you can fly after you get the stitches out next week. But remember, you still have the cracked ribs and are recovering from a concussion, to boot. Mostly, he recommends trying to take it easy for the next month or so."

I thanked the doctor, and as he left, the nurse began re-wrapping the knee. Again, I tried to remind myself of how much worse it could have been.

"You okay?" Will asked.

I could have handled it better if he had told a joke. Instead, though, the concentrated sincerity in his voice and eyes made my disappointment inescapable. Unable to trust my own voice, I responded only with a nod.

* * *

When we were back outside again, Will raised a hand to hail a cab, but I proposed walking, instead.

"I think I better take advantage of being out while I can," I said, trying hard to recover my voice and sound more upbeat than I felt, "before being holed up in Yinchuan for the rest of the winter."

He held out an arm in an "after you" type of gesture, then fell into pace beside me as I began my now practiced crutch-hop down the sidewalk.

"Sorry about Thailand," he said after a few strides. He paused, sounding like he wanted to say more.

I looked at him expectantly. Even from the little I knew of him I could tell he was mulling over some idea. Actually, Will was always pretty easy to read.

"It's just that, you know, there's really no sense in you going back up north to sit around by yourself in the dead of winter, right? I mean, you're in a vacation spot already. Some might say this is even better than Thailand. Beautiful weather, lots to do, plenty of cool people around … great Mexican food, of course."

In contrast to Will, I am often told that my expressions can be quite difficult to interpret. There is a seriousness that comes over my face whenever I begin thinking over the logistics of a situation, and I was no doubt projecting this now.

"I mean, you have to be here for another week, anyway, before you can get your stitches out," Will continued. "And then, if you can't travel, what's the rush in leaving? You haven't even really seen Kunming, yet. Oh, and we have a good bookstore."

When I still said nothing, he smiled again and added, "Just throwing it out there."

Once again, I thought about how quickly plans could change in China and how everything was starting to feel less about making decisions and more about just being able to respond. In many ways, it went against my strict athletic discipline and "high performing student" habit of detailed planning, but at the same time there was something practical, even attractive, about it. I wanted to be the kind of person who could respond to whatever life threw at me. And, what's more, I wanted to be around such a person.

"Hard to say no to a bookstore and Mexican food," I said finally.

"But that's the beauty of life," he said, raising his arms as if to take it all in. "We get to say yes."

CHAPTER SEVEN

~ *Springing Forward* ~

At my insistence, Will had promised that he wouldn't feel the need to entertain me during my stay. Availing myself of someone's guest room for four weeks without feeling like too much of an imposition was already going to be hard enough. And though Will had said that the restaurant could manage just fine without him, when we returned to the apartment, he made good on his promise not to rearrange his schedule any further on my account and headed off to work.

Left, then, to get my head around the new plan, I started by texting Kelly and Shaun, both to let them know about the proposed changes to my schedule and, perhaps, to give them the opportunity to talk me out of anything crazy. Instead, though, they found the plan completely sensible. Of course.

I wish I'd thought of it, Kelly texted. *Much better than being in*

Yinchuan by yourself. We'll see you in four weeks. Miss you! Have fun.

You, too, I wrote. *Hao da.*

Jihua meiyou bianhua kuai, Kelly finished. Plans can't keep up with changes. I began to understand why Kelly and Shaun had adopted and used this phrase so frequently. It seemed that this was not just an expression but a way of life that the three of them—Kelly, Shaun, and Will—had all taken to heart.

Next, I called the airline regarding my ticket to Thailand. I fully expected it to be a lost cause, seeing as I was supposed to be flying out in less than three hours, but they told me that while they couldn't refund it, they could make it open-ended, allowing me to use it anytime within the next six months. I didn't know if, realistically, I would get a chance to redeem it or not, but all the same it gave me a bit of hope. Maybe the airline, too, operated by the plans/changes way of life.

Having completed my two must-dos, I stood at the counter sink, poured myself a glass of water from Will's office-sitcom-style cooler, nearly identical to my own, and considered my next course of action. Remembering my guidebook, in spite of Will's earlier protests, I put down my glass, picked up my crutches, and hopped my way to "my" room, as I figured I should get used to calling it. When I returned to the kitchen a few minutes later and had lowered myself cautiously onto a chair, I flipped the book open to the section on Southern China. It was time to learn a new place.

* * *

Kunming, I discovered after a few minutes of reading the guidebook, was essentially a happier version of Narnia: instead of being eternally winter, Kunming's weather was described as eternally spring. Famously so, it seemed, to the point of earning it the nickname "City of Eternal Spring."

And, thumbing through the ten pages of listed attractions, it seemed there were plenty of other geographic and cultural draws, as well. There was something called a stone forest, and a set of caves with intriguing sounding names like the White Elephant, the Goddess, and the Lying Dragon. There was also the World Horti-Expo Garden, which I imagined to be something like a plant-themed Epcot. A flower and bird market, plus several parks, pagodas, memorials, and museums rounded out the list. It wasn't Thailand, but there would be plenty to keep me busy.

I continued scanning through the guidebook and stopped at the "Culture and History" section. One thing that had become painfully clear during my first half year of living in China was that I knew really nothing of its history. Despite telling myself that this was the year to ease up on the studying, to just relax and have a bit of fun, I knew myself well enough to know I loved a good research project. The consummate student, even then. And since I wasn't going to be bumming around a beach, I figured I might as well put the time to good use. Truth be told, this was probably more up my alley, anyway. I turned back to the beginning of the section and read the details on the first thing listed. I looked at my watch: just after one. With a determined nod, I stood up and prepared myself to head out. I was never any good at sitting around, anyway, crutches or not.

The City Museum was nearby—not more than a twenty-minute walk, even at my hobbled pace—and when I got there, the two young women at reception seemed overjoyed to have a visitor. They were also clearly very concerned about my condition. I assured them that I was fine, or at least soon would be, and proceeded to answer the usual questions with my usual answers: "from America," "teaching English," "in China for one year." After paying, I was given a pamphlet and directed upstairs with instructions to "please have a look." I thanked them and went inside.

The squeak of my crutches bounced around incessantly throughout the stairwell as I made my way up the one level, so when I reached the top and stopped for a moment to rest, the quiet was palpable. I hadn't realized until now that that was something I had gotten used to in China: the constant noise, so much so that it was almost eerie to be met with such sudden silence now. But it was nice, too, in that calming library-atmosphere sort of way.

My next realization was that I didn't actually know what there was to see here—the guidebook said only that it specialized in showcasing the city's history—so, before continuing any farther into the large room that looked something like a giant scrapbook my grandmother may have put together, I gave a quick look at the pamphlet in my hand. Finding a paragraph in English, I read:

> *Flying Tigers Exhibit*
> *Before the United States' official entry into World War II, many Americans sought to volunteer in the war effort. The 1st American Volunteer Group (AVG), based in Kunming from 1941 to 1942, formed a special division of the Chinese Air Force known as the Flying Tigers. This special exhibit honors their service.*

I put the pamphlet in my pocket and, suddenly becoming aware of a faint sound coming from behind a nearby partition, I followed it to find a small-screen TV with a John Wayne movie playing on it. John Wayne, depicting a World War II fighter pilot, was giving a heroic-sounding speech about sacrifice, and I stayed to watch a few minutes as he led a group of these Flying Tigers into battle. The good guys' planes, I noticed, were easily identifiable by the shark faces painted around their noses and by the cartoon winged tiger insignias decaled underneath the cockpit. In the movie, it looked like they were winning.

I saw this same design in several more pictures and posters of planes as I moved along the wall, and I read in the description beside one that the tiger illustration was done by the Walt Disney Company. I found it slightly unsettling, this clash of childish imagery and war, but there was also something very fitting about it, too, very American. It seemed an odd thing to make one feel nostalgic for home.

Farther on, I stopped at one photo showing several of these Flying Tigers soaring in chevron formation somewhere over the Himalayas, according to the description, and after studying it for a few minutes, I couldn't decide which I found more impressive: the precision with which these pilots were able to fly, forming a flawless V, or the fact that someone had been able to photograph it. Since childhood, I had held a fascination with how exact moments could be captured in time, be it through journal entries, books, poems, photographs, paintings, even the home movies and silly short films created by my sister and brothers and me with the family camcorder. Looking back, I suppose I may have always been destined to roam in the world of storytelling.

Pulling myself away, I squeakily crutched along farther down the wall until I came upon a couple of glass cases at the far end. A flight jacket lay open in each case, and when I got close enough, I could see that each one had a message sewn onto it, one jacket with it stitched onto the back and the other with it on the inside flap. The notes themselves were written in Chinese characters, so I turned to the small placard beside the first case and read the description:

The Flying Tigers were issued notes like this, known as "blood

> *chits," asking civilians to help them in the event of their being shot down. This blood chit reads, "I am an American airman. My plane is destroyed. I cannot speak your language. I am an enemy of the Japanese. Please give me food and take me to the nearest Allied military post. You will be rewarded."*

I took a moment to look over the jacket. It was heavily worn, made of brown leather in that classic bomber jacket style, and had several patches sewn onto the sleeves and left breast, but what caught my eye was that, in addition to the U.S. flag, the blood chit was accompanied by a second flag, a foreign one. It wasn't the red and yellow-starred one that I knew as the symbol of the People's Republic of China, the one I now saw multiple times a day; instead, it was red with a blue square and white sun. I knew I had seen it before, and after thinking for a moment, I remembered: it was the Taiwanese flag. In the literature that the agency had provided me with before coming over, there had been a section on political correctness in which I was advised to avoid bringing up anything to do with the history of "the three 'T's": Tiananmen, Tibet, and Taiwan. I had heard about the first one, of course, and I grew up frequently seeing bumper stickers that read "Free Tibet," so I could have guessed there was something political about that, but Taiwan … I had honestly never really thought much about it. I knew only that they produced movies and that, for some reason, its flag seemed to cause controversy wherever it went. And, yet, here it was on an American military jacket, accompanied by a plea for help. It seemed almost like something belonging to an alternate universe that I couldn't quite wrap my head around. I moved over to read the description beside the second case:

> *This blood chit reads, "This foreign person has come to China to*

> *help in the war effort. Soldiers and civilians, one and all, should rescue and protect him."*

Compared to the other, this one, it seemed to me, was strikingly sweet, reading as though in the tone of an older protective brother. But this, too, I found difficult to reconcile with the present.

After making it through the entirety of the exhibit, I looked again at the time and saw that I had only been in the museum for an hour and a half. With the crutches, though, it felt longer; I was spent. Returning downstairs, I thanked the women behind the reception desk, who again appeared thoroughly pleased by my visit, and headed back out onto the sidewalk. Earlier, Will had given me directions to an English used bookstore, so I decided to swing by there and get myself a book. Once I had the most recent Nick Hornby in hand, I returned to the apartment, settled onto the living room couch, put up my feet, took up my book, and promised my body it could be done for the day.

* * *

"Hi," Will said when he returned about two hours later to find me still on the couch, just having woken up from the sound of his coming in. "Looks like a successful day, following doctor's orders."

"Success," I said groggily, removing the book from my chest and rubbing my eyes. "I think I got everything sorted out with the airline and Kelly and Shaun. And I even managed to get out for a bit, bookstore and City Museum."

"Well done," he said as he set a bag of groceries on the coffee table and pulled the strap of his messenger bag up over his head. "I haven't even had a chance to visit the new exhibition myself, yet. Any good? But wait, before you answer: have you eaten?"

I hadn't, so we moved into the kitchen, and as he stood working over whatever dish he was beginning to prepare, with the aroma of spices slowly filling the room, I sat chopping onions and chives on a cutting board, telling him of John Wayne and the blood chits.

"Kind of strange to think about how it all turned out, isn't it?" I said, still trying to process all the snippets of information I had taken in from the display.

"You mean with China, after the war?" He lifted the cutting board that I had been working on and dumped the contents into a pot simmering on the stove.

"With China, Japan, the U.S., Taiwan … I don't know, I guess it just seems a bit sad when you think about how differently it all could have gone."

"Yeah, but who knows how things would have turned out if it'd gone any differently? It might not have necessarily been any better." He pulled the cornbread out of the oven and gave the pot another stir.

"Smells good," I said, now recognizing the smell of chili.

He took a bite off the wooden stirring spoon and nodded. "Anyway, I don't mean to sound like I don't think the Chinese got a rotten deal. They definitely did. They had a tough second half of the twentieth century, for sure. But things are getting better."

He dished up the bowls and brought them over to the table. "And, hey, we don't have to sew messages on our clothing anymore in order to survive here, so that seems a step in the right direction. Just a Foreign Burrito business card tucked into your running shorts, and you're good to go."

"Yeah, thanks to the kindness of strangers," I said.

"To the kindness of strangers … and allies," he said, raising his bottle of beer and tapping the top of it to the middle of mine. "*Ganbei.*"

* * *

Will's work schedule varied. He and his business partner, Roger, along with Roger's girlfriend, Mei (pronounced like the month), and two part-time student employees called Clinton and Blue, coordinated amongst themselves, alternating days and evenings. So the next day, being free until dinner, Will offered to assist in my new self-imposed educational directive and possible writing inspiration by giving me a lesson in "the influences of the West on China today." I had to laugh when I discovered that this primarily consisted of having lunch at a western-themed café called Happy Cup.

"I know," he said, acknowledging the campy décor as we took our seats. "But I actually do have a point here, which is that I would argue that this is as much a part of Chinese culture as anything else these days. People kind of knock it and say that this isn't 'real China,' but is it really all that different from, say, having a Chinese restaurant in Boston? Would you say that that isn't the 'real Boston'? Because we actually have a substantial Chinese influence in the city. The beauty of a place is in its evolution, brought by outsiders or by travelers who bring new ideas home. It's the reason pizza didn't stay in Italy and egg drop soup didn't stay in China and," he pointed to the menu, "whatever this is didn't stay in America. People back home like variety and trying new 'exotic' things; why shouldn't the same be true here?"

"But don't you think there's something lost in translation," I said as the Carpenters' *Yesterday Once More* played through the café's sound system. "I see your point, but don't you feel like sometimes what we end up with just feels like a bunch of ripped off ideas? A less good imitation of the real thing?"

"If we believe in survival of the fittest, we have to assume that the ideas will evolve with whatever attributes best help it adapt to its new environment," Will said. "Take Roger and me, for example. Two baseball-playing American boys making Mexican food in China. Of course, we've adapted the recipes to work here, just as they were adapted before us to make sense in whatever time and place we had it."

He paused, but I said nothing as I could see he was still formulating his thought. That was another thing about Will: he never steamrolled a conversation. He always gave plenty of opportunities for others to speak, even if they, or I, didn't always take them.

"Maybe my thoughts on food are similar to my thoughts on people," he continued after a moment. "The world is made of migration, humans moving and adapting, each generation and community blending cultures in a new, creative, innovative way. Who knows what might happen when you throw us all together? The possibilities are endless."

Our coffees arrived, and we both took a few seconds to inspect them. Mine had a cat face drawn in the foam, and Will's had a panda.

"See?" Will said. "The results can be beautiful."

* * *

I hadn't been back to the restaurant since my first day in the city, and with Will working that night and me feeling much better in regard to general soreness and the concussion, it seemed like a good time to try again. When I arrived, though, at about seven o'clock, I was unprepared for how different the place would be from the one lunchtime I had spent there. Gone was the quiet, empty space, and in its place I found a room buzzing with conversation and music. Will had come in earlier to help with the dinner crowd and now gave me a wave from behind the bar.

"Busy," I yelled when I had made my way over to him.

"Not too bad. Definitely some new faces—backpackers, I suppose, coming through on their winter holidays—but the usual crew is here, too." He saw Roger and Mei and waved them over. We exchanged nice-to-see-ya-agains, and they told me they were sorry to hear about the accident. They probably would have still been at work that day when Will got the call from the hospital. Quite the surprise, I imagine, to be serving food to a person one minute and, the next, to hear she's in the ER.

A good-sized crowd had now started to form around the bar, so, excusing themselves, Roger and Mei returned to their work.

"I'm fine," I told Will, still somewhat shouting. "I'll find a corner to sit in for a while."

"There's a good group up in the loft tonight," he said, with a nod toward the space above us. Then, glancing around, he spotted a middle-aged guy with long white hair, dressed head to toe in black, accessorized with a metal chain dangling from a belt loop to the wallet in his back pocket, and flagged him over. "Hey, West," Will said. "This is Anne. You heading upstairs?"

"Yup," said the guy called West. Then looking at me and noticing the crutches, he added, "Shit. What happened?"

"Road accident," I said. "But it's getting better."

"Doesn't surprise me," he said in the unmistakable drawl of the American South. "We get a lotta' accidents over here. But that is a bummer, for sure. Need a hand?"

Will gave a thumbs-up and returned to work as West took my drink and carried it up the stairs. I did my usual hop-step as I followed behind. When we reached the top, we were greeted by eight or so others, and taking a seat among them, I settled into introductory conversations while trying to piece together how each person fit in.

In addition to West, who offered no more information about himself other than that he did "a variety of jobs" and had been in Asia for "a number of years," there was Paddy, an Irish guy, probably late-thirties or so, who ran one of the used bookstores—the same one I had visited the previous day, as it turned out, though he hadn't been in at the time. Then there were Paul and Jen, both twenty-something, who taught English together at a primary school in a small town about two hours outside of Kunming—he with the British VSO, which I was told was something like the Peace Corps, and she as an independent Canadian; both just spending time in the city during the winter break. Rudi, maybe thirty, taught German at a local college and was, I learned, the newest regular of the group, having just arrived in China around the same time as I did. The remaining three, a couple of French backpackers and a girl from New Zealand who had just spent the past four months doing some sort of humanitarian study-abroad project in Myanmar, were just traveling through.

After the conversation bounced around for an hour or so, Paddy filled a momentary lull by returning to the topic of my injury, asking for more than the one-sentence explanation I had initially given. They all seemed interested in hearing the story, so I went ahead and told it.

"Must have been either a motorbike or a moped," Paddy said, after I finished. "That's the only thing that could have been going that fast other than a car and been small enough not to knock down anyone else. So, it's a good thing you kicked free of it; those motorbike engine burns can be nasty pieces of work. Recovery takes ages, too, and believe me, a

Chinese hospital is no place you want to spend very long in. Last year, I got a parasite and had to do a three-day stint. Three days of lying there, all hooked up to an IV … it was a pretty grim ordeal."

"I lucked out running into Will beforehand," I said. "I'm not sure what I would have done, otherwise, not being able to understand anything."

"If worse comes to worst, I think a person is meant to contact his country's embassy or consulate," Paul added. "That's what I've been told, in any case."

The two French backpackers leaned in together and discussed something between themselves in French for a few seconds. They had been doing this throughout the evening, helping each other translate, and this time, when they straightened up again, the woman of the pair said, "Yes, that is what we had to do, in Cambodia, two weeks ago. We were not injured, but our hotel room was broken into, and our passports and all of our money were stolen. Like you say, when it happened, we had no idea what to do. We couldn't even fly home. But finally, the hotel contacted the police, and the police directed us to the French embassy."

"That's like my worst nightmare," Jen said. "Having my passport stolen. But I've heard Southeast Asia's worse for that than here."

"I didn't have anything stolen in Myanmar," the girl from New Zealand chimed in, somewhat defensively.

Jen turned to her. "Well, I don't know about Myanmar, but I've heard the crime rate in Cambodia is really high."

"Well, generally speaking, in Asia, for *laowai*—foreigners like us—theft is usually the worst of it," West said, cutting through the tension with his drawn-out pronunciations. "Truth is, we stick out too much to be targets of any real violence; just watch your bikes, bags, and pockets, and don't do anything too stupid, and you'll be fine. Accidents excepted," he added with a nod at me. "Just keep your head up, and be ready to think on your feet, kids."

"I've had my bike stolen twice already," Rudi offered into the conversation.

"One of my students," Paul picked up, "told me he was late to class because he 'lost' his bike. I honestly didn't know what he meant at first. How do you lose a bike? But after pressing him for details, I figured out that what he actually meant was that it was stolen. I thought maybe he had simply confused the words, so I said, 'You didn't lose your bike; someone stole it.' But he just went on about how he must be more careful next time, as though he didn't want to admit that someone took it."

"Face-saving," West said knowingly. "If you lose your bike, it's an accident. No one's to blame. If it's stolen, it means you have thieves in your town, in your country, in your race, which is a shameful thing to admit, especially to a foreigner."

"Right, because none of us has thieves in our own country or people," Paddy said. "I don't know about you lot, but in Dublin, we don't lose our bikes—they get nicked by other Irish bastards. I'd say it's even a bipartisan affair." He finished off his beer and twirled his free hand in the air as though to say *que será, será*, whatever will be, will be. "Luck of the Irish won't help you there, fellas. Catholic or Protestant, young or old, foreign or not … shit happens to us all."

Standing to his feet, West added, "Well, damn, I'd say that's worth drinking to. To shit, the great equalizer. Who's in for another?"

* * *

"So," Will said as he lowered the metal shutter down in front of the restaurant and locked it into position, "you have fun up there with that crew? Some interesting folks, huh?"

"Yeah," I said, focusing on keeping steady on my crutches as I gave a wave to the back of Roger and Mei's departing taxi. Minutes earlier, I had sat watching the three of them, including Will, breeze through their well-practiced closing procedures. "They certainly have a lot of stories."

"Oh yeah," Will said, easily keeping stride with me as the two of us set off down the sidewalk, once again opting to walk. The apartment was relatively close, and it was another pleasant evening—eternal spring, indeed. Plus, after being inside drinking for the past few hours, it felt good to be out in the night air. "Stories for every occasion," Will continued. "One part news, one part advice, and usually about five parts one-upmanship. But anyway, it's good banter, as long as no one gets too pissed or political."

"I can imagine." I thought for a few seconds, then added, "It really is quite an unlikely group, though, isn't it?"

"Unlikely?" Will asked. He seemed to consider the word. "Hmm. How so?"

"Just in the sense that it's not a group I'd normally peg as being friends and hanging out together. The age range, the different nationalities, different occupations and ideologies … it's a little hard to imagine that they have many shared interests."

Will nodded. "Ah, I see what you mean. It almost sounds like the set-up to a bad joke, doesn't it? An Irish entrepreneur, a pair of young British/Canadian humanitarians, an old Southern rebel, and a couple of wandering backpackers walk into a Mexican bar in China …"

One of my crutches caught on a bit of uneven sidewalk, and Will put a hand on my arm to steady me.

"Thanks," I said. I did not like these things in the best of times, let alone after a few drinks. But it wasn't so bad with Will there.

"But there is something we all have in common," he continued in stride. "We're all here."

"Deep," I said.

"Not as in a 'We're all here on Earth' philosophical way," he said, smiling. "I mean that we're all here in China, in the same position of having left family, friends, and communities back home and are now having to create something new, a new sense of home, I guess. It might be a little like when stray dogs band together. Regardless of backgrounds and, as you say, as unlikely as the group may be, we're united because … we need each other. Even if people don't always want to admit it."

"The pack of the pack-less," I said.

"And all with the same patron saint: Saint Julian, watching over the wanderers of the world." He held up a medallion on his key chain. "Also patron saint of the circus carnies, I believe. So, you know, fallback career sorted."

It had not occurred to me that Will may have been religious. Growing up Baptist, I wasn't acquainted with the saints, but I knew something of the power of traditions and beliefs … and of the idea of something greater having a hand in our world. Of course, this wasn't the time or the place to delve into it, with me stumbling around on crutches on a Chinese sidewalk, a few pints in, so I said only, "Nice knowing someone's watching out for us."

"God knows some of us need it," Will said cheerily as we arrived at his building.

* * *

The remaining weeks passed quickly, too quickly. After getting my stitches removed and ditching the crutches, I spent most days exploring the city, on foot or with the aid of Will's bike. Will joined on the days he wasn't working, and on the evenings when he was, more often than not, I found myself at the restaurant, too, chatting with whoever was around that night. Sometimes it was just the four of us, Roger, Mei, Will and myself, finishing the remainder of a bottle of wine at closing; other times it was a loud, rowdy affair with the usual patrons and a handful of those just passing through. And some days, it was just Will and me, back in his kitchen, sharing stories from the day as he made something for dinner and I did my usual chopping. Whatever the case, I felt almost, for lack of a better phrase, at home. Except, I wasn't. Through all the easy conversations, easy day-to-day routines, easy time alone or with Will, I couldn't help but feel what I suppose can only be described as a measure of restraint. It was as though, while I knew that I had been accepted with open arms into the pack, the impermanence of it all made it hard to allow myself to delve in fully. And maybe Will felt it, too—a hesitation to appear to be taking advantage of what we both knew was to be a temporary situation. Whatever it was, in retrospect, it seemed that something was stopping both of us from making more out of those four weeks than what either of us had begun to feel they could be.

"Last chance," Will said over breakfast on the morning of my last full day in Kunming. He had an easy air about him, as always. "Whatever you don't get into today's exploration will just have to wait until next time."

"I know," I said, finishing my last bite of omelet. I tried to match his casual tone, despite my emotional somersaults. "So much pressure. But I think I've made up my mind."

"Alright then, let's hear it." He narrowed his eyes at the guidebook in my hand, skeptical as always, but resigned to my attachment.

I flipped open to the page and read, "With its mild temperatures and daily sunshine, it's no wonder that Kunming has earned the nickname 'City of Eternal Spring.'"

"Mmm hmm," Will agreed.

"It's also no wonder then," I continued, "due to these ideal conditions, that the city boasts Asia's largest …" I put down the book and looked at him. Of the several things I had learned about Will over the course of the month, one was that he couldn't resist a good guessing game.

He puffed his cheeks and gave a rapid-fire exhale. "I feel like I should know this," he said after another couple of puffs.

"It sells over two million of these a day, something people think of when they think of spring."

"Oh, the flower market!" he said with a snap of his fingers.

I nodded. "And, before that, I'm going to check out the horticultural expo. Seemed like a logical theme."

"Nice one," he said, standing and taking both of our plates the step and a half to the sink. He came back and split the remaining coffee in the French press between our two mugs. "And then, want to come back here, and you can tell me all about it over dinner? As long as you don't stand me up again like you did your first day here …"

"Jeez," I said, stopping mid-pour of the milk, "you're never going to let that go, are you? A girl runs off to the ER one time, and she never hears the end of it."

"Promises, promises," he said with that smile of his.

"Promises, promises," I echoed, unable to suppress a matching grin.

* * *

I set out, once again, one last time, on Will's bike, toward the expo garden, but for the duration of the ride I could only think about the approaching goodbye. Later, I would come to accept this as the simple reality of the transient life of foreignness, to see others and myself even become hardened to it, chalking it up to having a destiny where everyone just floated in and out of each other's lives, resisting placing any long-term expectations on oneself or others. But, in the moment, I just felt sad. I wasn't ready to leave.

By the time I finally arrived at the garden, I was in need of distraction and decided to throw myself fully into my surroundings. This had been a strategy of mine since I was little. My thoughts had a habit of running wild, but if I could contain them to a place, it helped sometimes. Thoughts with borders, I told myself. I bought the ticket, went through the turnstile, and looked at the map. There were areas with such titles as Plants and Technology, Plants from Around the Globe, Medicinal Plants, and Killer Plants, as well as drawings of plant sculptures in the shapes of dinosaurs, windmills, and castles. There was also a bamboo garden and a greenhouse full of *penzai*, which, judging by the picture, was the Chinese pronunciation of what I knew as *bonsai*. I pictured Mr. Miyagi teaching Daniel-san to harness his inner calm by trimming these tiny trees, and I wished I could have a moment like that now. In fact, the more I thought of it, the stranger it seemed that we, the pack of the pack-less both here and in Yinchuan, had so little input or guidance from anyone outside of our own generation when it came to our daily lives. There was West, and I supposed he could be seen as a sort of mentor … but, somehow, I doubted that he was looking to uphold such a title or responsibility. It would have surprised none of us if he were to simply vanish for five months without saying a word. And, of course, most of us had parents, maybe even grandparents still living, but how much input could they really give into the strange foreign lives that we lived here? With communication being limited to slow and sporadic sessions in some pay-by-the-half-hour internet café, or a note in a care package that could take three months to arrive, or, if one were really desperate, a prohibitively expensive landline call via pre-paid calling cards, we were, instead, mostly left to our own devices. It seemed to me that we had looked around for direction and had found only ourselves.

Catching myself and my thoughts running wild again, I tried to return to where I was. But being in a sort of man-made Garden of Eden seemed incongruous with my goal of trying to bring myself back into reality, so after a couple of inconclusive hours of physical and mental meandering, I decided to try my luck with another change of scenery by moving on to the famed Flower and Bird Market. It was located in what the guidebook said was the Old Town of the city, and, though it was a bit of a distance to pedal, when I neared, I could see that it was far from being a forgotten part of town: on the contrary, it was bustling.

Once I had chained up the bike, I started down a narrow street lined as far as the eye could see with birdcages, fish tanks, flowers, antiques, and other various knick-knacks. Then, coming to the end of that street, I turned down another, and then yet another. It reminded me of the giant home-and-garden shows my grandparents would take my siblings and me to at the Portland Expo Center each year—there was seemingly no end to the rows of koi ponds, water features, pergolas, and patio swings then, and now the maze of streets and alleys offering its wares seemed to similarly go on indefinitely. Both then and now, it seemed that most people, myself included, weren't looking for anything in particular—we just followed through the displays as they were laid out, passively taking in whatever there was to see. After passing through a few streets in this manner, I came to a giant multi-colored, plastic-panel-covered structure and stepped inside. Instantly, I became immersed in a world of fragrance, humidity, and color: row after row of tulips, lilies, roses, and daisies in every hue, in stacks and piles, filling baskets, potted, wrapped in plastic, sold as bouquets, all greeting me as though I'd just entered into the floral version of the Wonka Factory.

I joined a throng of people heading in one direction past a row of vendors and, after a few minutes of perusing, stopped in front of a table.

"*Duoshao qian*?" I asked—How much? I pointed to a small potted *penzai* tree on the table. It was, in fact, a whole miniature landscape, with moss and rocks and even a small figure sitting underneath the tree.

An elderly Chinese man, wearing the traditional Cultural Revolution-issued high-collared blue jacket, common among so many of the older generation, eyed me, nodded, and said, "*Sibai kuai*." Four hundred *renminbi*. Right around fifty dollars.

"*Tai guile*," I said a bit theatrically—Too expensive. "*Yibai*," I countered. One hundred.

He shook his head, also more than a bit dramatically, saying, "No, no, no," having switched to English, "I lose money at that price. Three hundred fifty." He typed the price out on his calculator.

This wasn't something I particularly enjoyed, this haggling process—I had never found it quite the thrill that others seemed to—but at least when it was done in Mandarin, I could tell myself that it was good language practice. Now, though, there was little I could do but play along and follow the expected script.

"I'm an English teacher," I said, smiling. "Not rich. One hundred fifty?"

"Okay, okay," he said, patting me on the shoulder. "Special price for you: three hundred. It's good price."

We both knew that a third of the original asking price would have been about right, but I had started too high, and there was nothing to be done about it now. "Okay," I said, "two hundred, final."

It was now his turn to smile. "Two hundred and fifty. Good, good." He handed me the pot happily as he could see I wasn't going to try to push him down any further. And he was right; other than when playing soccer, it simply wasn't in my nature to be pushy. I conceded, paid, and thanked him as I left.

Penzai in hand, I navigated my way back through to open air and was surprised to find that it was raining. It was just a few sprinkles, but turning my face upwards, I could see that a big gray mass was rolling in. There was more on the way, too, a lot more … and coming quickly.

I tried hustling through the narrow streets, retracing my steps to where I had left the bike, but I was clearly not the only one with the idea of beating out the rain. Walking shoulder to shoulder with a wave of pedestrians, I thought of how glad I was to be off crutches. Members from a senior citizen tourist group, hastily shepherded by their guide, cut across my path, and I stopped, waiting as they filed into a small restaurant.

By the time I reached the bike, the raindrops had grown to be about three times as large as when they first started and were landing twice as fast. So, after setting the tiny tree in the basket at the front of the handlebars, I unchained hastily and jumped on. If I hurried, maybe I could beat the worst of it.

I pushed off but then caught a glance down at the basket in front of me and quickly stopped again. I may not have known much about *penzai* maintenance, but I could see that with the jostling and pounding it was about to take, sliding around and being pelted by rain, it most likely wouldn't fare well if I didn't do something to protect it. In a few quick movements, I was down to a t-shirt, having wrapped my flannel overshirt around the plant. This delicate little thing, I figured, needed it more than I did.

Starting up again, I pedaled as quickly as my knee would allow, which I was happy to discover was reasonably fast, considering, and was certainly more than enough to keep pace with the surrounding bike traffic. Though the sidewalks had now almost entirely cleared, with the last of the pedestrians ducking into shops and under awnings, the bike lane was as packed as I had ever seen it. It seemed that afternoon commuters here, like anywhere, just wanted to get home, rain or shine.

In a matter of minutes, I was soaked through, and with paths of water running down my forehead and into my eyes, I could hardly see. Making a quick change of plans, I hung a right.

"You swim here?" Roger asked as soon as I had locked up the bike and dashed into the restaurant. He disappeared into the kitchen and emerged a few seconds later, tossing me a clean dishtowel.

I set the bundle on the bar and ran the towel over my face. "Pretty much. It hit just as I was leaving the flower market. Thought I'd stop in here to get out of the worst of it." I looked down at my dripping and now very dark gray t-shirt and khaki pants. "For however much good it'll do."

"Think it caught us all by surprise," Roger said, raising an eyebrow at the sopping flannel. Deciding to ignore it, he continued, "In the summer, these kinds of storms are more common—kind of like in Boulder—but this is pretty early in the year for afternoon showers." I remembered being surprised when I first learned that Roger was from Colorado instead of Massachusetts, where he and Will had met in college, playing together on the school's baseball team. By now, however, I was well acquainted with their passionate Rockies versus Red Sox banter.

He nodded toward the window and the weather beyond. "Clearly, though, flukes happen." Returning to the drippy mess lying on top of the bar, he asked, "Okay, I've got to ask. You try to rescue a stray cat or something?"

"Close. It's a *penzai*, aka bonsai, from the flower market. I'm not sure about its chances of survival, though, in all this."

"You might be surprised," Roger said, as I handed him back the towel. He tossed it behind the bar. "Sometimes the things that appear to be the most fragile are actually the most resilient."

I nodded. "That's kind of deep, Roger," I said with an exaggerated expression of being impressed.

"Yeah, well, Mei tries to teach me a few things."

Through the window, a plump middle-aged Caucasian couple caught both of our attentions as they bustled across the street toward the restaurant.

"Speaking of which," Roger continued, "we're going to see you tomorrow before you take off, right? I think Mei has a farewell gift or something to give you."

I promised I would come by just as the couple burst through the door, bringing a wet, electric energy with them. It was hard to tell if they had arrived deliberately or, like me, had merely blown in seeking refuge.

"Looks like we've got another couple of castaways," Roger said by way of welcome to the two newcomers.

The woman looked positively gleeful. "Oh, it doesn't bother us," she said in an American accent, shaking off her jacket. "We're no strangers to this kind of weather, are we, Jack?"

"Oh no, nothing we can't handle," the man, Jack, answered

in an equally amiable tone.

"We're from Florida—Sarasota," she continued. "Of course, our rain usually comes with a heap of lightning and thunder, fit to beat the band. I don't suppose you get too much of that here?"

"No, not many storms of any kind, really. I was just saying how this is pretty unusual, especially for this time of year," Roger said, grabbing a couple of menus and stepping over to meet them. "Anywhere you like," he added, waving a hand toward the empty tables. I wondered, in his line of work, with so many hours spent making small talk, just how many conversations he must have had about the weather, particularly here in a place famous for it. Yet, neither he nor Will ever seemed to mind. I was a bit envious, actually—what a relief it must be to feel you'd found your calling.

"So, is this your first visit to China?" I heard Roger ask as he followed the couple to their seats.

Knowing this conversation could occupy his time for a while, I indicated that I was going to head off and would leave him to it. The rain hadn't entirely let up, but the downpour seemed to have lightened at least to the point where I would be able to see.

"Will left maybe half an hour ago, so he should be home by now," Roger called out to me as the couple looked over their menus.

I gave him a wave and, taking my bundle, set back out into the city, homeward-bound.

* * *

When I arrived back at the apartment, Will was in the kitchen, already hard at work over the stove.

"You're soaked," he said when he turned and saw me.

"Like, wicked soaked."

I stood by the door, dripping, and pulled off my soggy socks. "Just a little rain. No harm done."

"Uh huh," he said, putting down his spoon and placing a lid over the pot he'd been stirring, "famous last words of William Harrison. Hold on a sec."

He crossed through into his room and came back holding a stack of clothes and a towel. "Here, put these on and hang those up so they have a chance to dry before tomorrow. We can't have you flying back up to Yinchuan looking like something the cat's dragged in, as my grandmother always says."

I wrapped the towel around myself and headed into my room. A few minutes later, I emerged looking like the runt of the University of Massachusetts baseball team, the words UMASS MINUTEMEN scrolled down one leg of the much-too-big sweatpants and the number five with two crossed bats stamped over the heart of a matching gray hooded sweatshirt.

"Hey, it's dry," Will said as I held my arms up to show the length by which the sleeves surpassed them. "And warmer than pretty much anything you packed. It's almost as if you were planning to spend your winter on a beach in Thailand or something." He was right; the only warm clothes besides the one pair of now-drenched khakis and the soaked flannel I had brought were a thin set of long johns and a mountaineering coat that had been easy to compress and pack once I had escaped the chill of the north.

He pulled two beers out of the fridge and held one up in inquiry. "Or would you rather have tea and whiskey?"

I held my hand out for the Tsingtao, and he popped the tops off both bottles and handed me one.

"Okay, real question," I said, looking around the kitchen to see if there was anything that needed doing. There wasn't. "Do you ever get tired of cooking? I mean, you're around food all day at work. You ever just come home and say 'forget it' and opt for a bowl of cereal for dinner instead?"

"My mother used to say that the kitchen is where she felt closest to God." He opened the oven door to reveal two beautifully browned circular sourdough loaves. "Which is saying a lot coming from a Catholic."

I handed him the pair of oven mitts sitting near me on the counter. I liked hearing Will talk about his mother. She had battled cancer for about a year before being taken by it while he was in college, but when he spoke of her, he actually seemed to breathe easier, like he could take a break for a moment and let someone else take charge. It also, I had learned, seemed more the exception than the rule, in this community, to talk about one's family with any kind of specificity. I couldn't tell if it was pride in trying to convince ourselves that we were entirely independent or if it was a sort of coping mechanism—perhaps if we didn't talk about them, we could help stave off thoughts of missing them. Or maybe people feared that it simply didn't make for interesting group chat; and, in this world, being responsible for bringing down the banter was a grave crime, indeed. At any rate, personal details of one's non-expat life, I found, were reserved for those you believed really wanted to know.

"There's something about the act of creation," he continued, gripping the tray as he slid the bread rounds onto a cutting board. He looked up and smiled. "Come on, you can't get this feeling from a bowl of cereal."

I returned the smile then watched as he cut a hole in the top of each loaf. I wanted to be able to imagine what life would be like if I lived here, really lived here, but it was difficult to picture. A month's long emergency convalescence, I told myself, was worlds apart from life with a regular routine.

"Okay, another question," I asked as he began scooping a

ladle-full of chowder from the pot into a bread bowl. "How long do you think you'll stay here?"

"Hmm, that's a trickier one." He paused mid-scoop, briefly, then continued. "Honestly, I don't know. I don't have any plans to leave any time soon, though, so maybe a while still. You?"

My offer for contract renewal, I had been told, would likely come within a couple of months, but trying to picture anything about the future seemed nearly an impossible task when there were still so many unknowns about the present.

"I don't know, either," I said. "It honestly seems like I just made the decision to come over here for this year."

Will carried our plates over to the table. "Goes fast, I know. But I usually find that the closer I get to when I have to actually make a decision, the more that decision just seems to kind of make itself. My trick," he said as we took our seats, "is to think of the options in the simplest terms. In your case, at the end of this year, you can either stay in Yinchuan, return to Portland, or move somewhere else. And you'll either continue teaching or do something else."

"Well, gee, that narrows it down."

He held up a hand. "Bear with me. First, think about anything you definitely want to rule out. For example, do you like teaching?"

I thought it over a moment. "Yeah, I think so. For now. Teaching or writing, maybe."

"Okay. And how about China? Do you like living here?"

"Yeah." I felt a sudden need to defend it, for some reason. Perhaps I was already thinking about what I might tell my family. "It's a big country. There's still so much to see and do."

"Well, there ya go." He motioned for us to begin eating. "At least you know you'd be fine doing this another year. That's a good start."

I took a bite, a perfect rainy-day meal, and struggled to put my fear into words. Finally, I said, "But what if there's a better fit?"

I always appreciated how well Will could think off the cuff and, yet, would take a minute to consider an answer when the occasion warranted. For me, it seemed that he was validating my concerns and questions, even if he had already come to some of the conclusions for himself.

"I think there are endless possibilities of what we could do," he said. "We could live so many places and have so many different experiences and meet all kinds of people. And perhaps we can do a lot of those things, but, no matter what, there is just no way we can do them all. So, to me, if you're happy in the here and now, what does it matter if there's potentially something else out there? I don't want to spend all my time on this earth, however long or short that may be, searching. Do you?"

"I don't know," I said honestly. Even then, I think I knew it wasn't just about what I wanted. "Maybe some people are just destined for a life of continual searching. Maybe that's the curse of the literature major," I said, trying to bring some levity back into the conversation. "There are infinite possible ways to interpret a story, and yet we doggedly read and analyze and debate, all to try to reach some definitive conclusion, which we know is ultimately unreachable. You know, now that I think of it, it could just be a major invented to occupy the insane."

Suddenly, in the way that ideas springboard from one to the other, talking about insanity reminded me of my sopping wet bike ride and the bundle I had left sitting next to the door. "Oh," I said, "I gotta get my … just hang on." I got up from the table and disappeared into the living room.

"A thank-you gift, for everything," I said, returning to the kitchen with the still-dripping flannelly mess. "That flower market had every kind and style of house plant you could imagine, and it went on forever." Leaning against his side of the table, I unwrapped the *penzai* and held it out between us. "This one might be a little worse for wear after the ride home, but, hopefully, it survived."

"Wow," he said, leaning in and inspecting the miniature details and figure under the tree before taking it carefully from my grip. "I've always wanted one of these. It seems so calming to just sit and shape it."

"That's what I thought," I said.

We were both quiet a moment as we looked closely at the tiny, vibrant leaves.

"I really love it," he said finally. "You can check on it the next time you're down. Make sure it's doing okay."

He smiled, then stood and added, "And I got you something, too." He strode into his room and returned holding a foot-long cardboard tube. He remained standing next to me against the table as he handed it over.

"Come on," I said in protest. "You already gave me way more than I could ever repay. A place to stay for a month, food … you literally rescued me at the hospital."

"*Mei shi*," he said with a wave of his hand. "It's nothing.

"The trick, though," he continued as I began opening the canister, "was thinking about what could travel. I hope it survives as well as the bonsai."

With that nervous energy that comes from a recipient unwrapping a gift in front of the giver, palpable self-consciousness emanating from both sides in close proximity, I pulled a scroll out of the tube and unrolled it to reveal an ink painting of a cherry blossom. The red and white flowers stood out against a blue sky, and a pagoda and Green Lake filled out the background.

"Something to remember us by. For now."

"It'd be pretty hard to forget," I said, looking up from the painting at Will.

"I know," he said.

He took a step, and I knew, too. Some things are just inevitable.

CHAPTER EIGHT

~ *Moving Forward* ~

Among all the other holiday adventures told and retold by returning students and faculty, my accident and the weeks spent in the south became just another one thrown into the mix, reveled in for a moment and then pushed aside as a new semester began.

For its part, the university welcomed us back with an announcement: a school-wide English speech contest would be held at the end of the second week of the term. The news was broadcast on a huge red banner overhanging the campus's central walkway, with a multitude of adorning streamers and fake flowers positioned underneath. To my surprise, the students seemed to greet it with genuine enthusiasm.

"A speech contest," I said to Kelly as the two of us walked under the banner on our way back from morning classes.

"Odd thing to get excited about."

Kelly had already grilled me about my time in Kunming and all about "this Will guy," so now we were back to commenting on whatever new daily events or observations popped up.

"Oh, it's a big deal here," Kelly said. "Bigger than a spelling bee. And this is just the first level. The winner from here goes on to compete at the city level, those winners go on to the provincial level, and then, ultimately, it's on to the national championships. It's government-sponsored, so there's a big to-do about it, lots of pageantry, song and dance, the whole shebang. Anyway, it's nice for the students to have something to look forward to."

"So, it's worth a watch, then?"

"Watch?" Kelly said with a cocked eyebrow. "You think they'd let the only foreign English teachers in the whole school get away with merely spectating? We're the judges, of course."

"Ah, right," I said, wondering when I might have found this out if Kelly or Shaun hadn't told me. It likely wouldn't have been until the day of the event when a couple of students would have shown up at my door to bring me in. It wouldn't have been the first time.

"The worst part about it is the length—it goes on for hours," Kelly continued. "But other than that, it's not so bad. There's nothing you have to prepare for, at least—just show up, listen, ask a few questions, and give a score."

We met up with Shaun, who had just finished playing basketball with some students. We headed to lunch where we continued the topic.

"Judging's really not that hard," Shaun said, signaling to the *fuwuyuan*. She hustled over with a notepad and took our orders. It was a soup noodles kind of a day. I thought briefly of Will's chowder. "It all comes down to tenths of a point," Shaun continued when the server had left, "and the range is pretty limited. For example, worst speech of the day? Six point five. Mediocre? Seven point eight. Most brilliant speech you've ever heard? Eight point six. So, whatever you give, you'll probably be in the right ballpark. But it's the questions that take a little creativity. That's the fun part."

"It honestly feels a bit like a game show," Kelly said as she poured our cups of tea, "or like a weird type of carnival."

Saint Julian, patron saint of the wanderers and carnies, I thought.

"Unpredictable and a little random," Kelly was saying, "but, hey, isn't that what we're here for?"

* * *

When the day of the contest arrived, Kelly, Shaun, and I were led to our seats in the front of the nearly filled several-hundred-seat auditorium, and each handed a pen and a stack of scoring cards. There was no mistaking our official capacity. Within a few minutes, one of the Chinese English teachers, Ivan, marched to the microphone at the center of the stage and gave the formal welcome. This year's theme, he announced, was *How to Create a Harmonious Life*. He then drew the audience's attention to us, the judges, which was met with a loud round of applause and brought a man with a giant video camera running down the aisle to position himself in front of us. He moved the camera up close to our faces for a few seconds until a pop song began playing over the sound system, at which point he turned again in the direction of the stage to film a group of students as they started in on a choreographed dance.

I leaned over to Kelly and whispered, "Are we supposed to score this?"

She shook her head. "These are the entertainment breaks, to get the crowd going and to help get us through the afternoon."

The dance was followed by a short skit about a novice tour guide in Beijing. We watched as the young guide gave nervous waves of her flag and made one comical English error after another while her gaggle of foreigners, dressed in matching hats, stumbled after her along the Great Wall and throughout the Forbidden Palace, growing more and more confused. Judging by the crowd's reaction, it was hilarious.

And then, suddenly, the first student was standing in front of the mic. She told us her contestant number and, without hesitation, launched into her speech. It was a fairly monotonous recitation—more like a well-practiced sales pitch than anything inspired or moving—but, nevertheless, it seemed to me that she did a fine job. She had a few clear points on how creating a harmonious life could be achieved by striving to get along with others, and her pronunciation was exceptional—better than most of my students, at least. In the end, she completed her three minutes without any glaring errors.

Shaun stretched his notebook across Kelly for the two of us to see. Across the top of the page, he had scrawled, "When has a stranger helped you?"

Kelly gave a thumbs up.

"Shaun will ask this one," Kelly whispered to me.

A student was rushing toward us with a cordless mic, and Shaun signaled for it.

"You say that to create a harmonious life, people should help each other in everyday activities and be kind to strangers. Has there ever been a time when a stranger helped you, and if so, can you tell us about it and about how it made you feel?" He enunciated each word carefully into the microphone. Free of Aussie slang, I realized, he could really be quite clear.

When he finished, the student, who had been leaning forward with an intense look of focus, smiled and gave a nod. She was obviously relieved to have understood.

"Thank you for your question, teacher," she said into the mic. She then gave a perfectly salient answer, which I noted in the listening and comprehension section on the scoring card.

"Okay," Kelly said, nudging me in the arm when the student had finished, "tally it up."

I did as I was told and arrived at a score of 7.9. I had no time to consider whether or not I was happy with this as a reflective grade as Shaun and Kelly were hastily passing me their cards and Ivan's waiting hand was already protruding out from the seat behind me. I handed all three cards to him and turned my head for a moment to see him recording the total in his notebook. I turned back toward the front when I heard the next student begin to give his contestant number.

This pattern continued, one student after another, with the occasional skit, dance, or song thrown in to help boost any flagging enthusiasm. For our part, in order to keep ourselves engaged with each speech at hand, Kelly, Shaun, and I began to hold a competition of our own, one that revolved around who could come up with the most creative questions. Anything related to the speech, we decided, was fair game.

You say that a harmonious life comes from taking care of the planet by recycling, turning off lights, and riding public transportation. Tell us, if you could make one new rule that everyone at the university would have to follow to help the environment, what would it be?

You say that a harmonious life is only possible if countries stay at peace with each other. But what can a college student do to encourage peace with other countries?

If having a harmonious life means enjoying yourself and relaxing with family and friends, what advice would you give to a person who has had a very difficult thing happen in their life?

We jotted these down in our notepads for each other's inspection, pointed to our favorites, and allowed the winner a turn with the mic—a dubious honor, undoubtedly, since the questions usually had to be repeated or reworded, sometimes to a student near tears, but still, it was a good feeling whenever a question of mine won out.

Finally, after just over three hours, the contest came to a close. Four finalists were beckoned onto the stage, and the places were announced: a tie for third place and then, with full dramatic flair as the two remaining students stood between Ivan, boxer-style, the runner-up and winner, with the winner's name being barely audible above the applause. I tried to recall the first-place speech: something to do with being a conscientious member of society. Nothing earth-shattering, perhaps, but certainly one of the better ones.

"Well," Kelly said as we packed up our things and prepared to follow the other teachers to a post-competition banquet, "you made it through your first speech competition. What'd you think?"

"Wow," I said, rolling my shoulders, stiff from hours of sitting in a hard wooden fold-down auditorium chair. "It's definitely got me thinking a lot about how to create a harmonious life."

"See, but for me," Kelly said as we began walking toward the door, "it almost has the opposite effect. After beating the topic to death all afternoon, doesn't it almost make you want a little conflict? Trying to maintain harmony all the time actually sounds kind of dull. Sometimes you've just got to disrupt the peace a little, pick a fight, mix things up."

Having just caught up to us and hearing only the tail end of our conversation, Shaun responded, "Uh oh, I don't like the sound of that."

"See?" Kelly smiled at me. "More fun already."

* * *

Would you rather have: a peaceful but somewhat predictable life … or a tumultuous but potentially more exciting one? I typed out the question on my phone that evening when I was back in my apartment, and hit send. I hadn't spoken voice-to-voice to Will in the two weeks since my return to Yinchuan, as even within-country phone conversations were pay-by-the-minute, but we had managed to keep up a pretty steady running dialogue via texting random observations and would-you-rathers back and forth, sometimes with days in between messages, other times only seconds. This evening, I saw as my phone gave a ping, it was the latter.

Do you mean: Do I think the fun is worth the crazy?

I began to type a response, but just then the phone rang.

"Sorry, but I had to know: Does this have something to do with your decision about next year?" Will said by way of a greeting.

"Hi to you, too. Just a sec," I said, leaving my lesson plans and papers scattered on the coffee table as I got up off the couch and moved across the room to the window. Pushing past the wall of hanging laundry, I took a quick hop and was soon perched up on the ledge. This had become a favorite spot of mine, a lookout post of sorts, and though the sports field was empty and dark at this hour, the city lights were as bright as ever. "It's good to hear your voice," I continued when I got settled.

"It's good to hear you, too." He paused, then continued in a tone similar to one I might employ in the classroom when trying to get wayward students back on track. "But this is not purely a social call, you know. I need to know what case to make here. Is this about you staying or not?"

"No." Then, rethinking, I added, "Well, maybe. But that's

not what made me think of it. It was the theme of the speech contest I was judging today, about creating a harmonious life. But, by all means," I said, shifting the phone to my other ear, "make a case for the crazy."

"Okay, I want to hear more about that, but, yes, first, I'll give you my theory in progress. A few years ago, there was this article about a woman who went skydiving and had her chute fail, mid-air. Somehow, she survived the fall, which was something like fifteen thousand feet, only to land right smack dab on a mound of fire ants and get stung over two hundred times."

"Jeez," I said. "Talk about bad luck."

"I know, right? It seems like the worst luck. Except here's the thing: as it turned out, doctors think that landing on the ants was actually what saved her because the adrenaline from the stings basically acted like a defibrillator, keeping her heart going until paramedics could arrive."

I made a sound of amazement, and Will continued, "So, after reading this article, I got to thinking about the physics behind it, the distribution of impact and that sort of thing."

"Of course you did," I said, my smile evident in my voice. I moved the phone again to my other ear, happy just to hear him talk.

"Then I came across Newton's Third Law of Physics—you know, the one about every action having an equal or opposite reaction—and it just clicked for me."

"O … kay," I said, dragging out the word and squinting out the window at the night.

"Like I said, it's a work in progress, but I think my conclusion is this: you know those Rube Goldberg machines, like the Mouse Trap game, where everything happens in order to set off something else in this really complicated chain reaction?"

"Sure, I've seen those. The science museum in Portland

had this big one when I was a kid where you'd drop this ball in and it'd trip all these triggers, which in turn would trip all these other triggers. I don't really remember what it accomplished, but it looked cool, at any rate."

"Right. So, my theory is that, although sometimes whatever is happening might seem like this unrelated or bad thing, like something might end up breaking and shattering into a million pieces, it's actually still serving a purpose, working toward something, which then sort of redeems it."

"And that something that it's working toward is … what exactly?"

"That," he paused, "I haven't fully worked out. But I like to think, ultimately, it's going to be something really amazing. Like, going back to the Rube Goldberg machine, it'll result in a super cool new way to make toast … but way better."

"A super cool new way to make toast? That's your case for embracing the tumultuous? Because at the end of it all, through all the ups and downs and things breaking and parachutes not opening and pieces shattering everywhere, the something greater at work, the point of it all is … that you end up with a super cool new way to make toast?"

"But way better," Will corrected.

* * *

"Give yourself time," Kelly said from her seat next to mine on the sports field bleachers. "By this time next year, you'll be a ping pong paddle racing pro."

The next starting pistol went off, and the boys' 200-meter dash was underway.

Unsurprisingly, I had only heard about the all-school sports meet a few days earlier when, instead of rushing out after class in typical fashion, my students stayed behind and began pushing aside their desks and chairs to clear space in the center of the room. When I asked what they were doing, one student, Meadow, told me in the sort of matter-of-fact tone that I had come to expect of my students, "We must practice our dance for the sports meet, teacher." It was sweet, really, how my students assumed that I, as a teacher, knew things, despite overwhelming evidence to the contrary. On more than one occasion, I had shown up for class to find my students had gone to some other scheduled event of which I had been wholly unaware, or had myself been suddenly whisked away and taken to some opening ceremony of a children's hospital or Women's Day banquet or some such thing, with my students never once feeling the need to offer or request explanation.

"So, you think I ought to stay another year?" I asked Kelly, applauding as a student of mine crossed the finish line and fell dramatically into his waiting friends' arms.

"Oh, I don't know. Must have been my subconscious talking," Kelly said, clapping absentmindedly as she scanned over the track and field. She pointed out Shaun, who was preparing to take a throw over at the discus event. "Which way are you leaning?"

"I've been going back and forth. Is it for sure that the school will even offer to renew the contract?"

"Oh yeah, if you want to stay here another year, you definitely can. The school will offer you the renewal at the end of April, and then the deadline for signing is a couple of weeks later, right after the May holiday."

We were both quiet a moment as Shaun took his throw. The disc landed at least twenty feet further than anyone else's. By my calculations, after my win in the javelin, Kelly's win in the high jump, and our team wins in a few of the relays, a win from Shaun in this event would push the English Department into first place. Happily, it didn't look like my poor performance in the ping pong paddle race would cost us, after all.

"It's all those years of playing rugby," Kelly said, nodding toward Shaun. "But," she looked at me, then continued, "well, I didn't want to say anything until it looked like it might actually turn into something … but it looks likely that Shaun and I won't be renewing our contracts for next year."

"Oh," I said. "That's … I didn't even … that hadn't even crossed my mind. What are you going to do?"

Kelly smiled at my stammering. "I know, we'll miss you, too. But we've both been wanting to go to grad school, and now, after three years here, it just kind of feels like the right timing. We've applied to a bunch of universities all over—Australia, New Zealand, the UK, Canada—and we figured that if either of us got in somewhere, we'd try moving there and giving it a go. And now, I've just heard back from one in Australia. It's looking good."

"That's great. Really." I gave her a congratulatory elbow nudge before adding, "Yinchuan won't be the same without you guys, though."

"Yeah, but you never know, our replacements could be okay. Or, of course, you could go elsewhere. Southern China, for example." She reciprocated my elbow nudge.

I reddened. "Yeah, maybe," I said. Again, I wondered if I'd ever view decision making as easily as Kelly, Shaun, and Will seemed to.

"For real, though, you should look into it," she continued, no longer teasingly. "You already know people down there, one guy in particular, and I'm sure they could ask around about a job for you. You said yourself how livable it was. Why not give it a shot and see where it goes?" Noticing Shaun walking across the field toward us and holding a first-place ribbon, Kelly held up her hands in victory. "And, hey, think of it this way: if we do all end up leaving Yinchuan, at least we're going out as champions."

* * *

"What do you think?" I asked Will that evening on the phone after filling him in on the day's sporting events and the conversation I had had with Kelly.

"Definitely. You could, for sure, master the art of the ping pong race by next year if you put your mind to it." His voice was accompanied by the sound of pots and pans clanging around in the background.

"A girl can dream," I said from my spot on the windowsill.

"Seriously, though, yes, I'm on it. I'll ask West about jobs—he'll know where there are openings and how to apply and all that. I'm sure he's even got his fair share of *guanxi* by now, so there should be a good chance. You finish up there at the end of June, right? So, we could maybe even do a little summer traveling in July or August. You still haven't made it down to Thailand, yet. Or Tibet's not too far. And you've gotta use that open-ended ticket they gave you, right?"

"Yeah, I was thinking about that. By the end of July, I think."

"Okay, and what about your family?"

Despite the fact that Will's and my family size and closeness were on different ends of the spectrum—him with only a maternal grandmother and his father, who had remarried and moved away from Boston; me with grandparents, parents, siblings, and cousins almost all living in the same area as each other—Will was nevertheless quite conscientious of trying to keep his friends from falling into the "out of sight, out of mind" mentality when it came to affairs back home. Perhaps he'd seen too many people forget where they came from and lose something of themselves. Or maybe it was just that, because of his loss, he had learned not to take family for granted.

"Have you talked to them about staying?" he continued. "And what about visiting home? I'm sure they'd want to see you this summer, sometime."

"They're actually okay. I managed to connect with my folks last night, and after I threw out a few ideas to make up for not seeing them this summer, including the possibility of them coming over to visit me for a couple of weeks either over the next October holiday or the winter break, they were supportive. They know it's a good opportunity for me to travel and build up my resume. Plus, they want to see the Great Wall, too, so they can save up the airfare for that. Win, win."

"Alright," he said. "Sounds like you've thought it out. I'll see what I can help get going."

"Like a Goldberg machine." I rubbed my sleeve to clean off a spot on the window. "Set things in motion and see where it all leads. The trap or the toast."

"Definitely the toast," he said. "But way better."

* * *

For the May holiday Kelly, Shaun, and I decided that instead of traveling elsewhere, we would spend it, as Kelly said, "exploring our own sandy backyard." Though none of us said as much, I suppose we all had the same idea: it might be our last chance.

And so, we went about soaking in all that the desert had to offer, from trekking the cliff-carved Helan Mountains to exploring seven-hundred-year-old beehive-shaped tombs to fan-boating on a lake famous as a stopover for migrating birds, the only place of respite amid the otherwise inhospitable landscape. We rafted the Yellow River atop inflated sheepskins, sand surfed, and rode camels and ATVs across the Gobi dunes; we ventured up along the border of Inner Mongolia, stayed in a yurt, and ate the fat of sheep's tails. And after getting windblown by gusts so strong they almost knocked us over, as well as being baked by the heat of the day and chilled by the cold of the clear starry night, at the end of the week, we returned to the city, having seen that the desert, too, can be beautiful. We also, all three of us, returned seeming to have come to peace with our decisions.

The first day back, I woke up at seven, as usual, in time to prepare for my 8:00 a.m. class. But when I pulled back the curtain of my bedroom window, I saw that something wasn't right. Or, rather, everything looked wrong. The air and light outside did not have the appearance of air and light, at least not any belonging to this world. Below, I could just make out the sports field, hazy and dull and cast in an eerily sepia-toned hue, as though being viewed through a layer of rust, and I stared at it for a few minutes, bewildered. But because I didn't know what else to do or who to ask—I knew Kelly and Shaun likely wouldn't be up as they had no classes until later in the day—I eventually turned away from the window and got ready, hoping to find an explanation from someone who knew.

Before I could get any answers, though, I stepped outside and immediately got a lungful of thick, earthy air, forcing me to retreat, sputtering back into the stairwell. As I braced for a second effort, I took note of my neighbors' strategies: with scarves or shirts pulled up over their noses, they tucked in their heads and slowly forged their way up the sidewalk. Doing the same with the collar of my shirt, I set out again, and this time, though visibility was still at a minimum, I could at least breathe.

When I made it to class, I was somewhat surprised to find that my students were actually there. I guess whatever was happening wasn't odd enough to force a cancellation.

"What is this?" I asked, employing as much animation as possible in order to cut through the lethargic mood of the class, which was likely due as much to the current phenomenon as it was to it being the Monday morning after a week-long holiday.

It seemed to work, and after the class had perked up and spent a few moments bent over electronic translators, I heard a couple of them reading out the word.

"Sandstorm?" I repeated.

Yes. It was because of the wind, they collectively explained—a strong wind from the north, perhaps from as far away as Siberia, would sometimes sweep down over the plains of Mongolia and across the Gobi Desert, picking up a cloud of sand along the way until eventually depositing it here, in Yinchuan. It only happens once or twice a year, my students assured me, always in the spring, and only lasting a few days.

I put my nose and mouth into the crook of my elbow and asked, "So, we will breathe like this for a few days?"

The students always seemed entertained by my charades.

"It is a pity that foreigners have such large eyes," one student said. "I think you will get quite a lot of sand in them."

After the morning classes, I headed to our rarely-used Foreign Teacher Office, a bare, small room we were certain was an ex-janitorial closet and which felt even more like one now with the musty smell of sand and lack of ventilation. Kelly and Shaun were already there, as we had planned to meet to walk to the FAO together. Today was the deadline for our contract decisions.

"Think we'll miss the sand when we're gone?" Kelly asked, stapling the last of her collated handouts.

"Don't worry, babe," Shaun said as he stood up from his desk. "Plenty of sand in 'stralia. We'll head out on walkabout when we need our desert fix."

Kelly smiled but, after looking around, she said, "You know, I'm going to miss this place, truly," and it seemed to me that there was already a hint of nostalgia in her voice.

After another moment, we took up our things and set off to give notice of our decisions.

* * *

When I got home that evening, I did as Kelly and Shaun suggested and stuffed towels around the windows and under the base of the door. Then I swept, dusted, and washed out my bowls and pots before making a simple rice stir-fry for dinner. Even so, by the time I finished eating and went to prepare things for my next day's classes, I noticed a thin layer of silt had already resettled on the linoleum. Ghostly-looking streaked footprints began appearing wherever I moved, sliding from room to room, stopping at every window and door crack where seals had been checked and re-checked. Clearly, regardless of all efforts, the sand would not be kept out.

When the phone rang, I knew it was Will, so I wiped off my spot on the windowsill and hopped up before answering. The air outside had now turned a deep red color.

"Hey, how's life in the land of eternal spring?" I answered.

"Beautiful, as always," he said. "And life in the desert?"

I spent several minutes recounting details of the day's sandstorm and effusing about the previous week's adventures in the Gobi.

"Sounds … cinematic," he said. "Any change of heart, then?"

It took me a moment to place myself back into the context

of his question.

"No," I said. "We all three told the FAO today that we wouldn't be returning. So, that's one decision officially made."

"Congratulations," he said. "And I actually heard from West just before calling you. He says he knows of a teaching job that recently opened up, if you're still looking at coming down here."

It was dark outside now, and I hopped down and pulled the curtains closed. One decision made, and already another needed. Maybe this is how it would be from now on. Maybe this was part of the deal: exciting but tumultuous. I thought of the two roads in Frost's poem, and the lines "knowing how way leads on to way, I doubted if I should ever come back" lingered a moment in my mind. Either way, though, at every junction, a direction must be chosen.

"Okay," I said. "Let's move forward."

PART TWO

~ SOUTH ~

CHAPTER NINE

~ *Crossing Boundaries* ~

The flight to Lhasa was scenic but bumpy. As I sat being jostled by sudden and, at times, violent bouts of turbulence, I kept my eyes fixed on the world beyond the window, trying to distract myself with Himalayan views. The densely clustered city of Kunming, which I had left a couple of hours earlier, had disappeared completely, and in its place arose a panorama of sparse, barren mountain peaks. With nothing else to claim my attention until arrival, I took a few deep breaths and began thinking over the events of the past six weeks. It felt good to just sit and breathe and think since, from that evening phone call when I'd first made this choice, it seemed I'd been doing everything but.

First of all, there had been the remainder of the semester: lessons to plan, finals to give—which were every bit as difficult to administer as the mid-term exams had been—grades to calculate, bags to pack, and, of course, travel and moving logistics to arrange. Then there were the farewells, a month-long process involving banquets and parties and nights of karaoke with every class and department, as well as goodbyes with all the shopkeepers and restaurant workers with whom I'd interacted on a regular basis and who had made Yinchuan what it was for me: home, if only for a year. I thanked Rose and Beckham especially for all their help and gave them each a painted scroll as a parting gift: a painting of a rose for Rose and, for Beckham, a humorous one of Chinese men wearing traditional dress playing soccer. In exchange, they gave me a giant red Chinese knot, a talisman of good luck.

Then, because there was no stopping it or even hitting pause, before we knew it, I was seeing Kelly and Shaun off at the airport, wishing them well for their upcoming Australian graduate school adventures.

"You're a bottler, Anne," Shaun had told me as he gave me a hug goodbye.

"I'm pretty sure that's a good thing," Kelly said, following with a smile and a hug of her own.

When I began to tear up, she added with an extra squeeze, "Hey, this isn't goodbye. We're going to meet up again. We're travelers—we never say goodbye. Just see ya later."

And though I smiled and said, "I know," as I stood there waving them off toward their gate, I knew I was saying goodbye. The inside jokes, the office banter, walks to the FAO, stories from the day's teaching, lunches of noodles, *jiaozi* or dishes with rice ... Kelly and Shaun had been there for it all, shown me it all, and I didn't know China without them.

But, in China, there is little time to reflect on a change; you were simply doing one thing one minute and something else the next. And so, after accepting the teaching job that

West had found for me, plans had immediately begun to take shape. Since the school would provide an apartment beginning in August, Will suggested that I move my things down to Kunming after classes finished at the end of June, and then he would take a few weeks off, and we could spend most of July traveling—except, of course, for the week of Roger and Mei's wedding, the date of which had just been announced. Will again posed Tibet or Thailand as possible places to visit, and since I had not had very good luck with Thailand the first time, I opted this time for Tibet.

Changes, though, once again cared little for our plans. After getting travel visas and booking plane tickets and reserving accommodations, on the evening of my arrival in Kunming and just two days before our scheduled flight to Lhasa, Will's grandmother passed away unexpectedly.

"Peacefully, in her sleep, at eighty-seven," Will said when he returned to the kitchen and told me the news. He had gotten the call from his father on the landline in his living room just as we had started our dinner prep, and, unsure of what to do, I had remained, fidgeting with the food.

"She had a great life," he continued, looking over the ingredients but clearly registering none of them. "Couldn't ask for much more than that."

She had been a sort of surrogate mother to him the first few years after his mother had died, and the weight of this new loss looked to be settling almost visibly upon him. There was no question about his attending the funeral. He had to go.

The ensuing conversation evolved quickly, practically. With so much to do, he needed to leave the following day. He would call the airline to arrange the flight home, and I would call to reschedule our Lhasa arrangements. Then, upon learning that the reservations we had made for the Tibet trip turned out to be non-refundable and non-changeable, and after hearing just how exorbitant a next-day ticket to the U.S. would be, I proposed that I could stay in Kunming while he went back to Boston for the week. This wouldn't accomplish anything, I knew—I would feel equally ineffectual whether I stayed in Kunming or went to Tibet—but it was the only thing I could think to offer. But, after hearing me out, he did what he always did: he made everything seem so simple. There was no sense in me waiting around here; he would go to Boston, and I would go ahead with our Tibet trip, alone.

"You're a good solo traveler," he said. "And what better place for someone always on the lookout for inspiration?"

I said nothing for a moment, thinking about how it wasn't the idea of traveling alone that bothered me but instead that it just felt wrong for me to go ahead with our plans without him.

"I know," he said, wrapping his arms around me and seeming to read my mind. "But it'll be okay. Everything's going to be okay."

And, at that moment, whether it would or wouldn't be seemed beside the point. For me, it was enough that he believed it for the both of us.

* * *

After the forty-five-minute bus ride from the airport into the center of town, I walked the few blocks to my hostel, checked in, then climbed the short flight of stairs up to my room, and, finally, collapsed onto the bed. Despite an acute sense of desperation coursing through my body as my lungs gasped for air and my head and heart seemed to race each other to be the first to explode, I tried to remain calm. I had read about this. Altitude sickness, according to my guidebook, is a common occurrence when first arriving in Lhasa, a city situated twelve-thousand feet above sea level. I would likely acclimate in a day or two, but until then, the advice was to "stay relaxed, keep still, and drink plenty of water". I would start by trying to breathe.

After about fifteen minutes, I felt recovered enough to try moving again, slowly, and started by making my way back downstairs.

"Hello again," said the young man behind the counter who had helped me check in when I first arrived. "I hope you are feeling better?"

"Yes, thank you. Just a bit tired." My head began to throb again as I glanced around at the small reception area, impressively crammed full of everything from an espresso machine and ice cream counter to several shelves of trinkets for sale.

"The altitude," he said. "Drink water, and go slowly."

I nodded. "Any suggestions for an easy first day outing?" Once again, I had accepted the fact that keeping still was simply never going to happen.

He pointed to one of the postcards in a carousel to the right. "Potala Palace. Very near to here. You can walk, and take it easy." Pulling out a map, he traced the route with a pen while circling a few other locations along the way. "But please, go slowly," he repeated. "Take many rests."

I thanked him and told him that I would. Running, of course, was out of the question, but I grabbed a business card for the hostel, just in case.

Outside, my eyes took a moment to adjust to the brightness, but when they did, the first thing I noticed was the abundance of tourists—Caucasian, Japanese, and Han Chinese, mostly, from what I could see. They looked the part with oversized, expensive cameras and fanny packs wrapped awkwardly around their persons, and I felt an immediate twinge of embarrassment, knowing that my foreignness lumped me in among their numbers. My initial reaction was to keep my camera and guidebook tucked away inside my messenger bag, as though keeping these things hidden would somehow help me blend in with the local culture, or stand out from these other spectators. But, after a moment, I realized I was really no different. Here, no one cared that I had lived in mainland China. I was clearly just another tourist. And so, taking out my camera, I slung it around my shoulder and tried to make the mental shift. As suspected, my actions garnered no difference in attention.

I soon reached what, according to the map, was the main plaza and, deciding to heed the advice of the hostel receptionist, found a spot on the plaza wall to sit and watch the world at eleven and a half thousand feet go by. In an instant, two young Tibetan women with babies strapped to their backs appeared in front of me, muttering and holding out their palms. Then, just as quickly, another foreign couple passed by, and the Tibetan women changed direction and headed off after them, instead. Watching the heads of their pink-cheeked sleeping infants bobbing against their backs as they went, I thought about taking a picture, then decided against it.

Out of the corner of my eye, I began to pick up on a certain deliberateness of movement, something swaying en masse and in sync. I turned to see a line of people, tattered and weather-beaten, walking in some sort of procession. When they filed past me, I saw that they were holding beads and something that looked like the little hand drum from the second *Karate Kid* film, the instrument used by Mr. Miyagi to teach Daniel to swing his arms back and forth across his chest. Upon closer inspection, though, I saw that, unlike Daniel's drum, these devices were made of metal and weren't making any sound, despite being spun back and forth in a similar fashion. Taking a moment to satiate my curiosity, I flipped open my guidebook and soon found the answer: so they were prayer wheels, mantras being spun around and around in Buddhist recitation.

Looking down the line of people, I noticed that it broke up, briefly, in front of a temple at the far end of the plaza. It seemed that each individual was taking a turn stepping forward and falling prostrate at the temple's entrance. Then, picking themselves up, the participants would rejoin the stream of people, which continued down the street before disappearing around a corner.

I wasn't sure what to make of it all other than that it clearly played some role in a demonstration of belief, a faith in the unseen or, at least, a searching for some hidden guiding hand. I continued sitting there, thinking of my upbringing, and of Will's, and wondering what Will's grandmother's funeral would be like. He had mentioned there being a wake, another tradition unfamiliar to me.

After being lost in thought for some time, I glanced back toward the temple and this time noticed that there were people—my people, the tourists—up on the roof with cameras, so I got up and, stepping around the prostrate worshipers, strode over to the entrance, paid the small fee, and entered. Making my way up the narrow, uneven staircase, I arrived at the top and was instantly blinded. Only by squinting and using one hand as a visor could I make out anything at all. It wasn't just the sun, I realized; it was the gold. The whole rooftop seemed to be covered in it: gold trim, gold statues, gold spires—all reflecting the sun from every angle. But, still continuing to shield my eyes, I soon made my way to the roof's edge, where, free from the glare, I could see the city. The plaza lay directly below, and beyond, rising up out of a nearby hilltop like a mythical Shangri-La, sat the receptionist-recommended palace. Framed by several surrounding mountain peaks and highlighted by a brilliant blue backdrop of sky, it did indeed look as pretty as a postcard.

It was a lovely rooftop view, but without beers and cards it wasn't a place where one could hang out for long. So, after taking a few pictures, I climbed back down the stairs and followed alongside the path of the procession making its way toward the palace. The street was lined with vendors, and as I moved along at my slowed-down, oxygen-deprived pace, I noticed several things for sale that were straightforward enough: trinkets, rugs, clothes, antique knives, and obvious foodstuffs. But there were also plenty of things for which I could not fathom the purpose or meaning: mounds of strange powders heaped onto blankets, dried lizards, bird talons, bogeyman-type masks, boxes with swastikas imprinted on the side … Whatever it all was, I couldn't shake the sensation of having inadvertently stumbled into the spirit world. I'd look it up later, I told myself. Especially about the swastikas—it was an unsettling thing to ignore, but at the same time, with the fatigue setting in, this seemed no time for reading. Instead, I decided to just keep moving.

When I eventually did arrive in front of the palace, I tried to let myself take it in, to be as impressed as I had been less than an hour earlier when I first glimpsed it from that golden rooftop vantage point. But, standing among the masses, these prostrating individuals engaged in something so obviously sacred, my uneasiness only grew. Anyway, it had been a full day, I decided as I turned to walk back toward the hostel. It was okay if I didn't see and understand it all in the first day.

After stopping for dinner at what I knew, but didn't care, was a café made for tourists and having a yak burger, milk tea, and a bottle of water, I made my way back to the dorm in hopes of expediting the acclimation process with a full night's sleep. Passing through the lobby, I walked by a notice board that I hadn't seen earlier and so stopped to check if there were any messages of interest. Most were notes from backpackers headed to Everest, looking for others with whom they could rent a Land Rover, either for company or to help keep costs down, I supposed. There were various dates for these proposed expeditions, but nearly all of them described the same route: planning to go one-way from Lhasa to Everest to Kathmandu. The thought ran through my head that it would be fun to see Nepal, seeing as how I was this close already, but considering time and visa constraints, I decided it best to stick within the borders of Tibet.

Still, a chance to see Everest was a hard one to pass up. And, almost as quickly as the thought occurred to me, I found myself tearing a sheet of paper from my journal and writing: *Lhasa-Everest-Lhasa. Return trip. One person seeks 3 or 4 others to rent Land Rover. Hope to leave* … I wrote the day-after-tomorrow's date, along with my name and number, and tacked it to the board.

* * *

At breakfast the next morning, I asked my new friend behind the counter what the best way would be for me to get a little outside of the city, to take in some of the countryside. He thought for a moment and asked if I wanted to see "a very simple town of farmers."

"Sounds perfect," I said.

He nodded, then wrote something down on a small scrap of paper and handed it to me. "The bus stop and number; I have written in Tibetan so you can hand to the driver." He then told me how much it would cost and gave me another business card for the hostel with the numbers of three different buses written on the back, any of which could be taken for the return. I probably would have thought his preparations a bit excessive except that I knew from experience that they weren't—here, our one-day relationship had suddenly elevated this receptionist to emergency contact status.

I waited outside for the number three bus, but when something resembling my dad's old VW van pulled up, I thought little of it until a teenage boy leaned out of the door, yelled something and, perhaps in response to my hesitation, reached around to tap a spot on the front window where the number three had been written on a piece of paper and taped up. Then, handing my own slip of paper to the boy, I got a nod and stepped on. Instantly, the boy shouted something again, this time to the driver, and we sped off. The only other two passengers, both elderly, watched me without expression as I took a seat, and we rode along in relative silence, punctuated only by the teenager's frequent shouts at whoever happened to be on the sidewalk as we passed by. Some took him up on the offer and climbed aboard; others paid no mind.

After about twenty minutes, it was clear we had left the city, for there was no one left for the boy to shout at, and no sidewalks left to pass. I sat staring out of the window at the surrounding brown hillsides and a few scattered houses until, after another twenty minutes or so, the boy called out something again and gestured at me.

As soon as I and a few other passengers had cleared the final step, the bus roared off again and left us in what I could now see was a small town much like the ones I was familiar with from back home: a one-road-running-down-the-middle kind of place. My hostel receptionist had certainly delivered—it didn't get much simpler than this. The other passengers all began walking in the same direction as each other, so I followed suit, keeping pace behind them until the few parties began splintering off down separate dusty pathways. Arbitrarily, I chose one lined with squat nondescript stucco buildings and turned down it.

I soon came upon a few dogs and children playing in the dirt, while a small group of women sat a short distance ahead, each on her own stool, and each washing her own item in need of cleaning: one washing her hair, another clothes, another cooking pots and some post-meal dishes. I hesitated, again acutely aware of my intruder status, but they only smiled at me and continued their work. Returning the smile, I walked past, and before long the houses thinned out, and I was surrounded by farmland. The first field I came upon was a patch of dark red dirt about the size of a basketball court with a farmer and yak working at plowing it under. Next to it there were several long, narrow plots, each stretching out one after another, covered in large sheets of black plastic with row after row of white- and green-leafed cabbage poking through. And further on, pretty much as far as the eye could see, swayed a large swath of yellow. It was not a crop grown anywhere near my hometown, but I recognized it from summer trips I had taken back to North Dakota as a kid, visiting the Scandinavian community where my grandparents had grown up. It was either canola or mustard. I took a deep breath of air. To be honest, I didn't care what the crop was. After a year of being surrounded by city and noise, newness and farewells, decisions and the unexpected, maybe silence, solitude, and a quieting of the mind were what I needed. Of course, I would have preferred not to have complete silence or solitude; I would have preferred for Will to be here. But, as it was, I just had to try to bounce ideas off myself. If I were going to be a writer, perhaps this was the cost of doing business—a lot of time alone in one's own head. Not necessarily what I wanted, but, as the Rolling Stones said, sometimes you get what you need.

I walked along in this train of thought, taking pictures and passing mud-brick homes, until at one of the houses a girl in a bright blue school jacket rushed up to me, took my hand, and began pulling me toward the door. The child's shouts sounded playful and inviting, and this was confirmed when, moments later, the mother came to the door and waved me in. Once inside, I was ushered toward a large bed, a bed so big that it filled half of what was clearly a multipurpose room, and was given the "have a seat and wait here" gesture as mother and daughter disappeared into an adjoining room. Moments later, the girl rushed back in and plopped herself beside me on the bed, beaming and chattering away. When I shook my head to indicate my lack of understanding, this only caused her to burst into fits of laughter. The mother soon returned carrying a thermos and mug and, after pouring the milky contents from the former into the latter, handed it to me. There was nothing for me to do but smile, thank her, and drink. Unlike the sweet milk tea I had had at dinner the evening before, this drink tasted primarily of salt and smelled a bit like bad milk. The mother seated herself on a stool next to a wood-burning stove in the middle of the room, and we all three sat there, smiling. I took another sip, trying to make myself think of it as soup—as opposed to the hot, sour, salty milk that it actually seemed to be—and found that that helped a little. Right, I thought to myself, swastikas and a salty milk drink: two things to follow up on next chance I have with my guidebook.

Suddenly, the girl jumped up again, saying something and pointing to the fire. When I made no response, she, still giggling, reached down, took up a round disc-shaped object from a stack next to the stove, cracked it in half, and put it in the fire. The mother said something, and the girl picked up another disc from the stack and, this time, handed it to me. I looked it over—it looked like a dried cake of hay.

"Like this?" I said as I emulated the girl by snapping it in half.

This, too, elicited laughter. Then, taking my hand, the girl, along with the mother, led me through the back door to the backside of the house. There, on the wall, sitting like splatter marks, stuck several of these disc-like patties. The mother pointed to the yak tied up in a small adjacent lean-to, then picked up a bucket with some hay and made a circular motion with her hands.

"For the fire," I said. "Good idea." I gave a thumbs-up.

They both beamed.

I wondered, briefly, if there were some point to this show and tell. But they didn't seem to be trying to sell me anything or to have me do anything in particular with this information. Perhaps they were simply showing me how they made fuel for the fire with yak dung and hay. Perhaps, like farmers anywhere, they were just proud of their innovation and wanted to show it off. They encouraged me to take pictures, which I did, and we returned inside.

Over another cup of the milky soup drink, the girl and I exchanged a few English words—"hello," "my name is," "from America"—followed by a few rounds of pointing at things with me saying the English words for them and the girl saying them in Tibetan, until after about half an hour, having thanked them profusely for their hospitality, I was on my way again, girl and mother standing in the door, smiling and waving after me as I went.

I wandered the side roads for another hour or so and then made my way back out to the main road. Unlike in Lhasa, I saw no other foreigners here, but other than the interaction with the girl and her mother and a few curious looks from passersby, I seemed to go mostly unnoticed, left alone in my wanderings.

Wanting lunch but not seeing any place obviously marked as a restaurant, I opted to enter the first open door through which I caught a glimpse of food. It was small, about the same size as the house I had been invited into earlier, and, for a moment, I wondered if I had mistakenly just entered into someone else's living room. A girl—eighteen, maybe twenty—was sitting on a nearby stool, slouching forward with her chin in her hands, absorbed in an Indian music video playing on a small TV near the back wall. To her right, with food in front of them, two men sat watching me without comment. Again, I had the feeling of being an intruder, but before my embarrassment could get the better of me and force me to turn and flee, a middle-aged woman came bustling in from another room and, with barely a glance in my direction, motioned for me to take a seat. She then barked something at the girl on the stool before hurrying back into the room from which she had just come.

I did as I had been told, as did the girl—or so I figured, because she got up and shuffled over to take my order. She nodded when I pointed to the noodle soup and fried bread that the men were eating, and I nodded when she pointed to their drinks. I couldn't tell if it was sweet milk tea or the salty one like what I'd just been served at the farmhouse, but as nodding and pointing were the extent of my communication abilities, I was in little position to be fussy.

From where I was sitting, I had a clear view into the side room, evidently the kitchen. The girl went in there after taking my order, and I could see her now, standing at a counter, beginning to chop chives. At the other end of the room, the woman who had come out a moment before was working with a lump of dough, quickly rolling it into a long white strip that soon grew to the length of the table. A third person, a man, stood near a stove, preparing a pan with oil.

I continued watching as the woman began pinching off small chunks of her dough strip, then pressing them flat between her palms and flicking them, frisbee-style, to the other end of the counter where they landed in a heap near the man by the stove. Spinning between the counter and stove and back again, the man moved with as much precision as a piece of machinery in an assembly line, rhythmically picking up the pancake-like dough rounds, laying them in the oil and taking them out again when perfectly browned.

After a few minutes, the girl came out with my bowl of soup, a thermos of tea—the sweet kind, I was happy to discover—and two fresh, hot flatbreads. I smiled my thanks.

* * *

I had no difficulty in catching the bus back into Lhasa—I likely looked like a lost foreigner in need of being returned to the city, anyway—and once back, with no plans for the remainder of the day, I returned to my spot on the plaza wall to enjoy the afternoon sun with some people-watching and, now that my head was a little clearer, more guidebook research.

Swastikas and salty milk, I remembered, flipping first to the *Food & Drink* section. The latter ended up being an easy one: butter tea made from yak milk, a Himalayan drink, popular for its warming and energy-boosting properties. An important tradition and symbol of hospitality, also supposedly good for altitude sickness. So, maybe that was why I was feeling better.

The swastikas, on the other hand, required a little more digging. Unsure of what section such a thing would be under, I first checked the index for the words "swastika," "Nazis," and "Hitler." No results. But I knew there had to be some explanation out there—I surely wasn't the first tourist to notice the startling prevalence of the symbol around town and wonder about the connection. I then tried a different tactic: after returning to the "S" listings and coming up empty for the word "symbolism," I decided to check the entries under "Buddhism." And there, sure enough, under the subsection "symbolism," I found it, both in picture and word.

The swastika, it turns out, is one of the oldest symbols in the world. Used in many ancient cultures as a sign of peace, prosperity, and general good luck, in Buddhism it is also meant to represent the heart and the mind of the Buddha. Brought into popular Western culture after the discovery of the lost city of Troy by a German archaeologist in the late 1800s, the symbol eventually became tied to German nationalism and an identification with an ancient, mythical master race: Aryanism. However, the paragraph concluded, in many Eastern cultures, the original meaning is retained.

Closing my book, I let my mind mull this over and wander through the things I had seen over the past twenty-four hours. The fact that some things could be interpreted with such vastly different connotations and understandings was a little hard to fathom. A symbol could simultaneously represent both peace and evil. A process could be routine for one and a complete mystery to another. Thinking about the people I had encountered—farmers with their simple yet effective technology, turning yak dung into fuel; teahouse workers operating with ultimate efficiency in their rhythmic bread making; pilgrims following a path laid out for them, diligently making their circuit in pursuit of some higher plane—it almost seemed as though we were living in alternate universes, functioning under completely different sets of rules. And I wondered if we all, in some way, envied each other. Did the other's rules and paths seem, if not better, at least clearer? Did people in the other universe have life more figured out? Then, again, I wondered which was ultimately better: knowing your role and fulfilling it without the inefficiency of hesitation and uncertainty, or believing that you could be and do anything if only you could decide, bouncing around confusedly in the meantime? As Will had pointed out once, I would likely be fine doing any number of jobs and living in any number of places, including teaching English in China. But was this it then? Was this the decision that would cement my future, or would I, as seemed so common the case in this transient world, simply do this for a while before drifting in a different direction? Faced only with more possibilities, not fewer, would I have to go through this every year? And each time, would I be consumed by wondering if this was what I was meant for … or if there was something else … or if I even believed in such a thing as fate or purpose? I just wondered if I'd always feel so lost. And again, I wished Will were here to talk it through with.

Suddenly, my existential introspection was disrupted by a sharp noise. It took me a moment to realize that it was my phone, which now, after the quiet of the day, seemed much louder and more piercing than necessary. But I answered: it was about the note that I had left on the hostel's corkboard. The caller was there at the hostel, so I went to meet him, arriving a few minutes later. The guy, a Canadian college student, I quickly learned, was waiting in the reception area along with his Swiss girlfriend. Additionally, they were joined by a young, newlywed American couple whom they had just met and who was interested in the trip as well.

"Okay, we've got our group," the Canadian guy said. "What's the plan?"

It took me a moment to realize that this was directed at me. Usually, Kelly and Shaun or Will, the expat pros, figured these things out, and I was just along for the ride. But with this group, I was no longer the newbie; instead, having lived not yet a full year in China, I was suddenly viewed as the one with the answers. I was, of course, responsible for our being together—I had written the note, after all—but, until this moment, it had not occurred to me that people might actually turn up.

"Okay," I said. And then I did the one thing that I knew worked, or at least what had worked now twice before: I asked the receptionist for suggestions. True to form, he gave us the name of a travel agency down the road, and we were off. By early evening, it was settled. We would leave for a four-night round-trip journey to Everest the next day.

* * *

When the Land Rover pulled up in front of our hostel the next morning, the five of us piled in, arranging ourselves by size: the tall Canadian up front, the other three in the middle, and me, the smallest at 5' 5", in a sort of fold-down jump seat among the luggage in the back. We knew from our travel agent that our driver spoke no English— "But rest assured, he does know the way," she had said in what sounded like a joke she had told many times before—so once inside, we simply flashed him a thumbs-up and were on our way.

The scenery for the first several hours was much like that of the small town and farmland I had seen the day before, and we passed the time, after the initial standard travel itinerary talk, with a hodgepodge of conversation topics. We talked about freeing Tibet, which none of us really understood but, nonetheless, managed to have some opinions on, to Texas's supposed right to secede from the Union, an idea that the American guy was all in favor of because, in his words, "they could keep their President Bushes and nut-job conservatives to themselves." We learned from our phones and cameras that batteries died quicker at higher altitudes and discussed, cluelessly but enthusiastically, why this might be. We then collectively wondered if lungs, once acclimated to high altitude, would adjust easier the next time. Of course, we didn't have the answers to any of these quandaries, but we were early- to mid-twenty-somethings—a lack of knowledge wasn't going to stop us from theorizing. Plus, it helped fill the time, so no one seemed to mind.

It wasn't until about three hours in when, much like the turbulence on my flight into Tibet, the bouncing and jostling inside the SUV became impossible to ignore. True to our travel agent's word, the driver clearly did know the way and had driven it many times before, but this seemed only to make matters worse. Over the increasingly mountainous road, he sped along, completely unfazed and unslowed by the boulder-size holes, sharp turns, and steep drop-offs that lined our way. Similarly, he was completely unconcerned with his cargo, that being us.

When the road had first begun to get volatile, our reactions were like those one might see or hear elicited at an amusement park: a group of riders letting out a thrilled, collective gasp with each roller-coaster-like dip. Gradually, though, as the jarring intensified, we stopped laughing, and stopped talking. Whether this was due to an increased nervousness or due to getting the wind repeatedly knocked out of us, it was hard to tell. At one point, when another jolt sent me, along with all of our surrounding luggage, crashing into the ceiling then down again with a thud, the bouncing even drew blood: I received two perfectly symmetrical small cuts in the top of my head where my sunglasses had been sitting.

When we stopped for lunch at what seemed to be the Himalayan equivalent of a truck stop, our driver went into the back of the restaurant, presumably to eat with people he could talk with, and the five of us were seated and brought tea and fried rice, which were apparently the only things served. We were then left alone to try to regain our sense of equilibrium.

"I think I need a cigarette after all that," the Canadian said. "You guys mind?"

After a year of living in a constant haze of Chinese cigarette smoke, I hardly noticed it anymore and shook my head no. The other two girls did the same.

"Please, blow it this way," the American guy said. "I think I picked a bad time to quit."

The Canadian took a long drag and slumped back in his seat. "It probably won't do my lungs any favors at this altitude, but at least it'll help with the nerves."

The Swiss girl, looking somewhat nauseated, pushed her plate away and leaned back beside her boyfriend.

"My god," she said, "this road is crazy."

"Obviously takes a crazy son of a bitch to drive it, too," the Canadian added. He set his cigarette in the ashtray and took a few bites of rice. "But better him than me. It'd probably take us a week to get there if I were driving."

The American girl, digging through her camera bag, said, "I'm going to take some Dramamine and see if I can sleep through the rest of today's drive. Anybody else want some?"

"You'll miss the scenery," her husband pointed out, matter-of-factly.

"With another eight hours of this again tomorrow, I think I'll see plenty," she said as she pulled out a blister pack of pills and popped one out. She offered them around, and the Swiss girl took her up on one.

The American guy shrugged and stretched his arms against the back of his chair.

"Gonna be worth it, though," he said, adjusting his neck side to side.

"Absolutely," the Canadian said, surrounding us in a haze of smoke.

* * *

We stayed the night in a remote guesthouse that felt like it could have been an alternate setting for *The Shining*. Other than the receptionist, we saw no other people, be they townspeople or guests, but with its location halfway between Lhasa and Everest, I imagined it had to have seen its fair share of travelers throughout the years. Maybe it was just a slow night. Or late or early in the season. I realized I really had no idea when the peak season to visit Everest was or even how many visitors Everest typically got each year. I recalled someone telling me, or maybe it was just something I had read, that the Nepali side was the more popular of the two base camps, so maybe everyone was over there. Anyway, with the guesthouse as quiet as it was, the five of us chatted amongst ourselves over another meal of fried rice and spent the rest of the evening in our six-bed dorm with a few beers and a pack of cards, always Hearts, until around eleven when we called it a night. With the couples pairing off together, both sets pushing their single beds next to each other, I lay in my bed alone, listening to my headphones and staring at the ceiling, the remaining empty bed in my periphery. I think I fell asleep after a couple of hours.

The next morning, having survived the night, we picked up where we'd left off, tumbling along in a cloud of dust and bumps. The American girl turned out to be right: the scenery was much the same as the day before, at least for the first couple of hours. Then, suddenly, having just come through a pass, our driver pointed and drew our attention to the peak straight ahead. There, though its top was obscured by a blanket of clouds, stood what we had come to see: Everest. I immediately began thinking of how I would describe it to Will. If he thought the rooftop views in Lijiang were amazing, how much more would he love this?

We drove along for several more hours, a mountainside to our immediate left and a thousand-foot drop-off to our immediate right, until we came to a small, isolated outpost, an out-of-place concrete fixture, sitting forlornly alongside the narrow dirt road. Again, I wondered how the Nepali side was faring. Having been told by our travel agent what to expect, we quickly paid the fee for our entry permit into the national park, then proceeded, heading straight toward the mountain until, by late afternoon, we had reached the end of the road.

* * *

We pulled up to a large building and parked alongside four other black Land Rovers identical to ours. A prominent wooden sign declared that we had arrived at Rongbuk Monastery—at 5,009 meters, the highest monastery in the world.

"Almost sixteen and a half thousand feet," the American guy said, looking at a GPS device he had taken out of his backpack. "My goal is to make it to eighteen thousand tomorrow."

"What's that in meters?" the Swiss girl asked.

"Nearly fifty-five hundred," he said.

"Perfect," the Canadian guy said, pulling out his pack of cigarettes and offering them around.

"Better lungs than mine," he said when no one took him up on one.

As we stood waiting by the car, per our driver's instructions when he went inside to make whatever arrangements he was making, a middle-aged foreign couple, the first tourists we had seen on the trip, appeared from around the corner of the monastery. Spotting us, they strolled over.

"Survived the drive. Congratulations!" the man said in an accent that, by this time, I was quite familiar with: Australian.

We made small talk about the trip, and having just come in from base camp earlier that day, they gave us a few pointers, describing the hike in and the conditions we could expect at the camp. The locals referred to the mountain as Qomolangma, they informed us, and we should wake up early, around dawn, if we wanted to get a clear view of it before the clouds rolled in.

"Oh, and stock up on chocolate bars here before you head out. It's pretty sparse out there," the woman added.

Just as the couple had sauntered off, our driver returned, waving us away from the back of the SUV, and began unloading our bags. Having worked it out with our travel agent before leaving, we knew what the plan was: our driver and car would stay at the monastery while we, accompanied by local guides, would walk the four kilometers to base camp to eat and sleep and spend most of the next day exploring around the mountain. The next evening, we would return to the monastery where we would stay that night, then begin the drive back to Lhasa the following day. We knew all this, but still, our driver seemed skeptical, either doubting our grasp of the plan or doubting whether or not we would adhere to it. He took out a pen and notebook from the glove box and wrote down "9:00 AM" and the date for the day after next. He then tapped the paper with his pen and pointed down to the spot on the ground where we were currently standing. We nodded and gave several thumbs-up. Yes, we would be here, in two days, 9:00 a.m., we assured him through pantomime.

Two guides with donkeys appeared and tossed our packs into their respective carts, then beckoned for us to follow. I almost felt bad for our driver as we nodded our goodbyes—maybe he had had passengers go rogue before and had spent countless hours waiting, vacillating between annoyance and worry like a father of teenagers out past curfew—but, at any rate, we were out of his hands now. We were entering the world of the mountain.

After an hour, the seven of us, plus the two donkeys, arrived at a small, dusk-lit tent village. The sun had dropped behind the mountains about halfway en route, so we tipped our guides and, deciding to save our explorations for the daylight, settled on calling it a night in one of the large canvas tents propped up around us. The one closest to us had a hand-painted sign above the entrance reading *Hotel California*, and that was enough to entice us in.

Dinner, like all the previous lunches and dinners of the trip, consisted solely of fried rice, but we made no complaints. Perhaps it was the altitude or the long days of travel, or perhaps being as remote as we were, our minds had simply kicked into survival mode, but whatever it was, we ate as though it were either our first meal or our last for a very long time. Then, having satiated that need, we immediately turned our attention to the next: protection from the elements. When the sun was shining and we were keeping active on the hike in, we needed only our t-shirts and khakis, but now, in the dark, hemmed in by mountains and ice, we discovered it didn't take long for temperatures to reach a biting cold. Finally, after adopting a tactic involving the putting on of several layers of clothing, draping sleeping bags over our shoulders, wrapping hands around mugs of tea, and sitting huddled as close to the wood-burning stove in the center of the tent as was possible without setting ourselves alight, we succeeded in achieving a modicum of comfort. At any rate, we were warm enough to play a few quasi-distracting rounds of Hearts.

Before bed, we made efforts to brace ourselves for taking turns, one by one with the aid of a flashlight, going behind the tent to administer to our toilet necessities. When my turn came, I jumped up, pulled the sleeping bag off from around my shoulders, grabbed the flashlight, and dashed out of the tent flap. But, instead of being struck by the cold, it was the darkness that consumed me. Flicking off the flashlight, I stood, frozen by the absolute and all-encompassing nature of the void. It was as though the night air had swallowed us whole. And each of us was utterly alone.

***

The fire died sometime in the night, and I lay awake, now acutely conscious of three simultaneously true absolutes: utter darkness, utter cold, and utter isolation. I shivered and could think of nothing else until, finally, hope arrived in the form of the smallest slice of dawn. As it crept through the slit in the tent flap, I took a moment to get my bearings, then slipped out of my sleeping bag, put on my shoes, and stepped quietly outside. Picking my way over the rocks as I looked for a spot away from the tents to sit and watch the sunrise, I heard a wristwatch alarm go off and knew that the others would soon be making their way outside as well. But, even so, it seemed it would make little difference—in this expanse, we made little impact on the landscape, whether one of us or twenty. Taking a seat, I watched as my first unadulterated, cloud-free view of the peak began to come into light. As I think of it now, it replays almost as if it had been one of those time-lapse nature videos, except I know that this happened in real time: the mountain, at first nothing more than an indistinct blue-gray silhouette, suddenly transformed, turning from vague shadow to golden-crowned to fully aglow, all in under a minute. And, as the surrounding landscape brightened also, something else became clear. We had, in fact, not been swallowed. We were still here, victors over both the dark and the cold. As for isolation, perhaps it was more of a truce.

After a simple but welcome breakfast of sweet milk tea and bread with jam and butter, the American guy pulled out his GPS and showed it to us.

"Okay, we're currently at sixteen thousand, nine hundred feet," he said. "That leaves eleven hundred to go. Who's up for it?"

I had no other particular agenda for my time up here, and neither, it seemed, did the others, so we all got ready and set out for a trek along the glacier. We soon forded one small stream and then another and scrambled up a few boulders here and there—all in all, not that different from a mountain hike back home, I thought at first. But here, there was little talking, and conserving our breath seemed more and more critical with each foot of elevation gained. After about an hour, I changed my mind about it not being that different from home. Home had trees, evergreens as far as the eye could see, with a green, dripping canopy above and a spongy trail of pine needles, dirt, and tree roots below. And no scarcity of air. Here, the only signs of vegetation were the few scraggly twigs of scrub brush. The rock-hard ground and surrounding air offered nothing—no give, no life. The only similarity, really, between a hike at home and this was the motion, the act of putting one foot in front of the other, traipsing across rock and earth in pursuit of some particular end.

"Success," the American guy said after we had been at it for a few hours. He held up his GPS as though preparing to plant a flag. "Eighteen thousand, two hundred feet. I think we can officially call that pretty damn high, don't you think?"

"My lungs are fucked," the Canadian guy wheezed in response.

* * *

Back at the monastery that evening, I don't know which we were more excited about: the fact that we had all just been to the highest point on Earth that any of us would probably ever get to, or that after a couple of days of subsisting almost exclusively on fried rice and Snickers bars we were now holding menus with the words "wood-fired pizza" listed on them. We ordered one for each of us.

"I've died and gone to heaven," the Swiss girl said after the food arrived and we had each taken a warm, gooey bite, cutting through strings of cheese with our teeth.

"Pizza on Everest," said her boyfriend, already nearly done with his first slice. "Kinda weird, but also amazing."

"That's all I want in life," the American girl said. "Kind of weird and kind of amazing."

"You're kind of weird and kind of amazing," said the American guy. His wife smiled at him.

I had wondered if we would see the Australian couple here again. The mountain was big, of course, but it seemed that maybe it was much like how the rest of China felt, that there were only so many places a visitor was likely to be. With a quick scan of the nearly empty common room, though, I saw that the only other patrons besides us were a handful of drowsy-looking Chinese tourists who seemed quite content not engaging in conversation. Equally content, we ate our pizzas, and afterwards skipped the card games to retire to our respective bedrooms dispersed throughout the monastery's various hallways. The building itself was modest, to say the least, yet with walls and a roof to protect us from the unforgiving elements, it felt almost like a fortress. Alone again with my thoughts, I fell into a sound sleep.

* * *

The high spirits from the previous evening continued into morning when we all gathered at breakfast, and after our bowls of muesli were eaten and cups of instant coffee drunk, we set off again, ready for the journey back. At first, the ride was uneventful, quickly passing through the scenery we had been in just a couple of days previous. But then, with the abruptness of a swiveling lighthouse beam, the glistening reflection of a windshield focused our attention up ahead. It should have been just another SUV filled with tourists, an unremarkable black rectangle silhouetted against a brown and gray backdrop of the surrounding mountains. But, by the askew angle at which it sat across the road, facing us in uneasy stillness, it was clear that this was something deviating from the norm. Something in this scene was wrong.

Slowly, as we drew nearer, the scene revealed itself. A group of three men, Japanese, middle-aged, stood together near the edge of the road, each with his head craned, trying to get a view of something at the bottom of the canyon. At their feet, two dark scars cut into the earth, bending opposite to the road's curve.

My fellow passengers must have worked it out at the same time as I did because, suddenly, the air inside our vehicle went completely stiff. Just for a moment. Then, in what seemed to be one continuous motion, our driver jerked up on the handbrake, threw open the door, and jumped from the car, leaving the rest of us frozen to our seats. As we looked on, he and another man, presumably the driver of the other vehicle, spoke and gestured wildly, punctuating the air around them with flailing arms and urgent Tibetan. Darting to the edge, they pointed and continued their animated discussion while the five of us inside the car remained motionless.

The group of three, still standing where they had been when we arrived, seemed to be at as much of a loss for what to do as we were. Slowly turning and lifting his head, one of the men locked eyes with mine, and somehow that look told me: Death had arrived.

Of course, it's easy to look back now and think that perhaps this should have been taken as some kind of omen, a warning of more tragedy to come. But, in reality, even if it had been, how could one have known the changes in direction to take? Instead, for each of us, we cannot avoid what we do not know … and, as it was, at that time in my life, I knew nothing of death. I had had no real proximity to it, and any understanding I did have was solely as a concept, a sad but inevitable aspect of humanity explored, in my case, primarily through literature.

This, then, is the only explanation I have for what ran through my mind as I sat on that return road from Everest, transfixed by the expression of a stranger: the lines from Hamlet's famous soliloquy. *For in that sleep of death, what dreams may come, when we have shuffled off this mortal coil, must give us pause* …

Suddenly, as abruptly as our driver had vacated the car, he returned and began yelling and motioning for us to get out. The three in the middle seat slid out in a matter of seconds, and I scrambled out after them, climbing over the headrests in front of me, then falling hard onto the ground outside. I felt a sharp pain in my left knee, the same one I'd injured in the accident a few months before, and looking down, I saw the reason: I had landed directly on a knife-point corner of a rock. But it was of little consequence now, so I got up quickly and stood with the others, watching as our driver climbed back into the vehicle and drove, in reverse, down the road and away from us. He continued like this for a few hundred feet until he came to a section of road wide enough to maneuver a turn, and then, with quick, efficient movements, he did so and began speeding off in the direction from which we had just come.

"He must have gone for help," the American girl said to no one in particular. "That little outpost probably has a radio."

None of us responded. Instead, with quiet understanding, the five of us walked along the tire tracks toward where the group of Japanese men stood. We passed the other driver, but he, too, was now quiet and kept his eyes fixed on the ground.

When we got closer to the edge and were standing near the three men, I asked if they spoke English.

"A little," said the one whose pained expression moments earlier had conveyed so much. In broken English, he proceeded to tell us probably all there really was to say: the two cars had surprised each other speeding around the blind corner from opposite directions, and one had lost control. It was, of course, believable—we had gone flying around these same corners ourselves, expecting and seeing no one—but standing there, looking out over the side, knowing that the overturned vehicle lay crumpled on the rocks a thousand feet below, I found myself searching for more of a reason than just unlucky timing. Lowering myself to my knees, I leaned forward enough to look straight down the rock face, trying to study the scene for clues—the crushed Land Rover, black like ours; the metallic undercarriage, broken and exposed; the still, dry ravine on which it lay—then my acrophobia got the better of me, hitting me with a wave of vertigo, and I was forced to take several shuffling moves backward. If the others, like me, had been looking for answers, they too seemed to come up empty because for several minutes no one made a sound.

"They must be dead," the Swiss girl said finally. Then, perhaps realizing the needlessness of her comment, she added, with a look toward the Japanese men, "Did you know them?"

The men shook their heads, and somehow I found this even sadder. It seemed the least that we, any of us, could do was to feel a sense of loss for whoever was down there.

"I wonder if we did," I said. "If not known them, we may have at least met them. Seems possible since they were coming from the mountain just a little ahead of us." I thought through the few people we had seen at base camp, plus the Chinese party and the Australian couple at the monastery.

"Could have been a group coming from Kathmandu," the Canadian guy said, in what sounded like an attempt to make us feel better. "Probably not anybody we had talked to."

In the end, I knew it made no difference. I nodded as I tried not to picture anyone's face.

Climbing down the cliff face was clearly out of the question, and with nothing else to do, one of the Japanese men took out a packet of cigarettes and offered them around. We each took one. I noticed that my hands were shaking.

I took a puff of the cigarette and watched the smoke rise, then did it a second and a third time. It seemed strangely empowering, as though flipping a middle finger toward both life and death.

The American guy inhaled deeply from his cigarette and then, holding it between his index and middle fingers, pointed with it in the direction from which the Japanese party had come. There, in the distance, was another black Land Rover, hurtling toward us, toward the mountain. I looked at the Japanese party's driver standing near his vehicle and felt sorry for him. He would soon have to tell this all again.

***

Not much had changed when our driver returned about two hours later, except that the road was passable again, the driver for the Japanese group having pulled his vehicle up ahead to allow the other expedition to get through, and the eight of us were now sitting away from the ledge, leaning against the rocks on the opposite side of the road, me with a flannel shirt tied around my knee. Other than the one vehicle, no one else had passed by, and we had continued to say very little. Our driver spoke briefly again with the Japanese group's driver, presumably telling him that help was on the way, and then herded us back into our car. As we set off, I turned to look back at the Japanese party, but none of them looked up. I supposed they would need to wait to give some sort of statement.

For the remainder of the day's drive, there were no more talks of politics, Texas or Tibet, and no more wondering about batteries or lung capacity. Instead, we moved along silently. Maybe, like me, the others too were trying to shake the mental images and what-ifs running through their minds. Soon, though, I was reminded of the throbbing pain in my knee and looked down at the makeshift flannel bandage. Unwrapping it, I first inspected the shirt—not too much blood. Then, I looked over the tear and dried bloodstain in my khakis—not unsalvageable. Finally, rolling up my pant leg, I saw that the gouge, hitting right at the top of the diagonal scar left by my previous accident, was really quite deep.

"You okay?" the American girl asked, having turned to look out of the back window and noticing me.

"Yeah, fine. Just fell on a rock, but it's not that bad." I fished a tissue out of my bag and dabbed it with water. The blood had formed a long, dry, red streak down my shin, having already run, I supposed, before I had thought to tie it with the flannel, bleeding as I stood smoking by the edge, taking no notice.

"Looks pretty bad," she said as the others joined in turning to give it a look.

"I'll take care of it when we stop tonight." It seemed a trivial thing to be talking about after the day's events, so I rolled my pant leg down and was glad when they all turned to face forward again and let the subject drop.

We stopped again to stay the night in the halfway town, though this time arriving a couple hours later than planned, and picked unenthusiastically at our plates of fried rice as we talked, with an equal lack of enthusiasm, about what we each planned to do after our return to Lhasa the following afternoon. The Americans were heading home; the other two would continue traveling throughout China, making their way east and then north, on to Beijing; and I would fly back to Kunming. After dinner, while the rest of the group started in on what I imagined would be a rather subdued game of Hearts, I followed our driver across the road to a small shop for bandages and antiseptic. The shopkeeper and driver chatted for a few minutes, probably about the accident, then turned their attention toward me.

"Sorry, sorry," the shopkeeper said to me in English.

Whether he was apologizing for the accident, the wound, or for keeping me waiting, I couldn't tell, but all the same I responded automatically, "*Mei guanxi.*" *It doesn't matter.* After I said it, I realized that nothing could be less appropriate if indeed he had been referring to the accident, but he seemed not to notice, either way. Moving about the store, he simply collected the supplies I needed while the driver and I stood watching. It occurred to me that perhaps there just isn't a good response to the word "sorry" in any language.

Back at the guesthouse, I started cleaning and bandaging

the wound and saw that my initial assessment was right: the cut was deep, and without stitches, it would scar. But as my mind began replaying scenes of the wreck—the upturned vehicle, lying small and crumpled at the bottom of the ravine; the dark tire marks cutting into the dirt; the cliff face, steep and impassable; the pained expression of the Japanese man—I hurried to finish, wanting only to put the entirety of the day's events to rest.

* * *

Late the next afternoon, we arrived back in Lhasa and unceremoniously said our goodbyes before disbanding and heading off in separate directions. We most likely all felt the same way: we had lives to get on with. I think I knew even then that, after those five days and four nights together, we would never see each other again. In fact, after we parted, I would not even be able to recall their names.

For my part, after arriving back into town, I stepped into an internet café and began writing a couple of emails: a brief one to my parents, followed by a group one to my collective siblings, updating them all on my whereabouts—in Tibet, headed to Kunming in the morning—but I stopped short of writing anything about the accident. My family had been ostensibly supportive of my wanderlust, trying their best to hide any apprehension they might have felt at my being halfway around the world in a place so different from home, and I didn't see the point in alarming them now. Accidents could happen anywhere, at home as well as here, I told myself as I sent off the second of the emails. I then read a short one that had just arrived in my inbox from Will. He was on a layover in Taipei. The funeral had gone well, a nice service, a good turnout, a fitting tribute to his grandmother. He should arrive in Kunming in a couple of hours, he said, and would be at the airport tomorrow when I got in. He reminded me that some friends were visiting for Roger and Mei's imminent wedding, so the apartment would be a full house.

I wrote my reply, expressing that I was glad that things went as well as could be expected at home. "I just arrived back from the Everest trip," I added, but then paused, fingers over the keyboard, unsure of how to continue. Unlike with my family, I knew that my hesitation now was not because I was concerned about worrying him—he had already seen me bloodied and semi-conscious in the ER, after all. Instead, perhaps it was that the form of communication itself felt inadequate. Perhaps I just wanted to talk to him, to hear him explain how his crazy Goldberg mousetrap theory could make sense of it all. Or maybe I just didn't want to continue thinking about these weighty topics alone anymore. I looked at the clock: he'd be boarding in a few minutes.

"There's too much to write about now," I wrote instead, "but …" I took a breath, trying to push myself to be something I knew I wasn't, to say something about how I felt without first analyzing all the possible implications and consequences. But it was no use. I settled for "I can't wait to see you tomorrow," then restated my flight details, though I knew he already had them, and told him I'd try to get ready for wedding party mode. After hitting send and logging out of my account, I walked to the counter to pay for my thirty minutes. All around me, teenagers were playing video games.

Back at the hostel, I got ready for bed but then lay awake, staring at the ceiling. I remembered the Canadian guy telling us the first day, sometime during the lung discussion, that he'd read something about how altitude affected people's sleeping patterns and dreams, and I tried to convince myself that this could be what I was experiencing. But, of course, I knew it was much more likely that, without any other external stimuli to distract me, my thoughts simply had nowhere else to go but to return to those same images: the crushed Land Rover, the tire tracks, the thousand-foot drop, the look on the face of the Japanese man … I began to wonder if the victims had been identified yet or if anyone even knew enough to miss them. Perhaps the driver's family had been told, but it seemed very possible that the news had not made its way across whatever oceans or landscapes it would need to travel to reach the respective passengers' homes.

I forced myself to think of something else. I began thinking of the mountain before the accident: that first night outside the tent, being engulfed in darkness, feeling swallowed by it, disoriented and alone. I focused on that, on the pitch dark, then gradually allowed for the appearance of stars, imagining their arrival coming like pinpricks in a black canopy, one after another. In my mind's eye, I zoomed in on one configuration, picking myself out as a single speck of light. My family I saw as a far-off cluster, Kelly and Shaun as shooting stars blazing across the sky. And there, in the tiny dots surrounding me, were Will, Roger, Mei, and the rest of the Kunming crowd, making up the constellation of which I now found myself a part. It was to this image that I finally drifted into sleep, imagining us all there, shining for a moment in the same spot of sky.

CHAPTER TEN

~ *Navigating Humanity* ~

On the ride back from the airport, Will was the first to acknowledge his frustration over our current time and energy constraints. The wedding was now only three days away, and with hosting duties and activities it would likely be a little while before we could catch up properly.

"But I want to hear all about everything and about this accident and just how you're feeling."

"I know," I said, leaning against him in the back of the taxi. "I want to hear about how you're doing, too. But for now ..." I closed my eyes and exhaled deeply, feeling the muscles in his arm tense and release as he pulled me in tighter.

"We embrace distraction," he offered.

"And, hey, it's for Roger and Mei—no better cause, right?"

"Definitely."

We sat like that in silence for a minute, until he tapped my arm and said, "Hey, I just remembered a joke that one of my grandma's friends told at her funeral, and it reminded me of you. She prefaced it by saying that she came from old Norwegian stock, so even though she and my grandmother had been friends for more than sixty years and had seen each other through all of life's ups and downs, it would be difficult for her to put into words all that their friendship had meant to her. She said, 'Maybe you've heard about the old Norwegian farmer that loved his wife so much he almost told her. Well, that's how it is with some people. Betty was one of my closest friends, and, though I may never had said as much, I loved her and will miss her dearly.'"

"That's really sweet," I said. "And, hey, it may have taken sixty years, but she got there in the end. Guess that means there's hope for any of us."

"Well, for now, we just have to make it through this next week."

"Deal," I said.

* * *

For all of Roger's American friends and family, this was their first visit to China, and all of us, expatriates and Mei's family alike, despite most of them also being from out of town, seemed to take it as a matter of collective responsibility to show them a good time and present the country at its very best. In addition to the planning of and partaking in several local and traditional Chinese meals, our time revolved around the coordination efforts of leading various groups on outings to parks, markets, and museums around the city. I couldn't help but feel as though we residents had all become something like a group of co-parents, concerned only with ensuring a safe and successful series of created memories for our dependent charges.

For their part, Roger's family and friends were good-humored and spiritedly joined in whatever was presented to them, but even so, when we arrived at The Foreign Burrito and everyone was seated for the night-before-the-wedding dinner, it was with a clear measure of relief in the air. Roger and Mei's worlds had come together—the foreign and the familiar—and both had remained intact, with neither being diminished by the other. A question held by both parties, it seemed, had been answered.

When everyone was finished eating, Will called our attention by standing and tapping a fork to his glass. The place was packed, but after making his way to the front of the bar, he made sure to position himself where even those in the balcony could see and hear him.

"On behalf of Roger and Mei," he began, projecting his voice in an enunciated manner, much like the style I had learned to adopt when speaking in the classroom, "I want to thank everyone for coming tonight."

As he proceeded with his best man's speech, describing how Roger and Mei had first met—she had become a regular at the restaurant in its first year, studying Chinese poetry and English translation as a senior in college—I thought about how comfortable he looked, how natural, and how naturally people responded to him.

"So, the next time Mei came in," he was saying, "Roger was ready. There she was, up in the loft, drinking her coffee, book in hand, when he mustered up his courage, walked up, took a breath, and declared …"

It was a perfect choice of story, just the right notes of funny and sweet, a literal lost-in-translation moment when Roger confused the Mandarin words for "salty" and "like," and the room reacted accordingly. Listening to the shared laughs and *awws*, I realized that I had unconsciously begun to feel a sense of pride. Maybe I wasn't entitled to it, but I let myself feel it, nonetheless. For as many uncertainties as there were in our lives, I loved that Will was always sure to come through.

"But luckily," Will continued, clearly nearing his conclusion, "Roger is never one to be down for long. The next day, he tried again, and the rest is history."

After a delighted round of applause, Will quieted us once more by raising his glass. "So, this evening," he said, "on the eve of their marriage, I would like to propose a toast to these two: *Xian Xin* and *Lajiao Xin*—Salty Heart and Spicy Heart. The perfect pair."

More toasts and speeches followed, but to be honest, I hardly took notice of any of them. When Will returned to his seat beside me, I wanted to think of nothing but being where I was, happy in the moment, alive, my hand in his.

* * *

The apartment, with a few of Will and Roger's friends having spread out over the living room for the week, had taken on a sort of frat house ambience, and none of us were getting as much sleep as we probably should have been. Nevertheless, even after staying up half the night drinking and talking, I made it to Mei's by ten the next morning, ready for the day, as instructed.

I had been told beforehand that this was the custom, for the bride's party to meet at her home while the groom's met at his, and while I hadn't been given many details, I was glad to have been invited to Mei's. I had heard that, at the very least, it promised to be the livelier of the two.

Still, I was mildly surprised when I arrived and was

immediately yanked inside, being instantly absorbed into the packed and raucous atmosphere. I appeared to be the only non-Chinese here—Roger's friends and family were going to the groom's home—and so was thankful to be guided by one of Mei's roommates to a seat on the couch alongside Mei's mother, grandmother and two aunts, all of whom I recognized from the past days' activities. I smiled and, per usual, in order to make up for my lack of language abilities, began looking for ways to demonstrate my enthusiasm. Being handed a bowl of peanut noodles and a plate of hot buns with sweetened condensed milk dipping sauce, I tucked in with gusto.

At about half past ten, Mei emerged from her room and, like much of the previous evening's proceedings, was heralded by a roomful of applause. Well-deserved adoration, I realized, when I stood and was able to catch a glimpse of her through the crowd. Dressed in a slender floor-length red and gold peacock-feather embroidered dress, Mei looked truly stunning.

And then, just as quickly as I had been pulled inside, we were once again moving out, bustling en masse out the door and down the stairway. I had been told that we would journey on foot to Roger's apartment, a twenty-minute walk away, but I could not have imagined just what a spectacle we would make until I saw what was waiting in the courtyard. At first, I couldn't make sense of it. Then I realized, the thing that looked like a British telephone booth with poles coming out the side was actually a bright red sedan chair, trimmed and tasseled with gold, and would serve as Mei's ride.

After taking a seat, Mei was hoisted above us like an empress, her four uncles and cousins manning the poles, and, in our best imitation of a royal procession, the whole lot of us began parading down the street. Someone handed me a present to carry, another set off a noisemaker, and everyone began shouting in celebration. Even passersby joined in with echoes of congratulations of their own. It was contagious, this jubilation, and it reminded me of when my family and friends worked themselves into a frenzy while cheering on the Seahawks. There was a freedom in giving yourself over to the loud excitement of the collective; and it was certainly more enjoyable than the alternative.

And so, in this way, we carried on down the street until we reached Roger's place. And then, again abruptly, we went quiet, adopting an air of formality as we arranged ourselves into a single file line to be greeted and bowed to, one by one, by Roger's family and friends. Will, I could see when I got in line, was one of the greeters, and he gave me a smile and a bow as I passed. I returned both and made my way inside.

Once there, I moved toward a spot near a back wall and could not imagine how we would all fit inside. But, somehow, we did, squeezing in until the last of us had been welcomed. Then, thankfully, we began to flow back out again. Will caught up to me as we were ushered outside, and soon we were all standing shoulder to shoulder in the courtyard. This, I realized as we arranged ourselves to face toward the center, was where the ceremony would take place.

It was brief: vows and gifts were exchanged; several red envelopes changed hands; more bowing ensued; and, then, just like that, we were on the move again. Except, this time, instead of an adorned chair, there was a procession of black cars, each draped with red and gold ribbons, awaiting us in the street. After Roger and Mei climbed into one with their parents and grandparents, the rest of us found seats in the remaining cars, and we were off, car horns blaring.

I knew when we arrived at the restaurant and made our way past the fish tank and into a private room at the back that we were in for a full-scale banquet. The room, too, was decorated wall to wall with more red and gold: a variety of intricately woven decorative red knots, as well as red and gold streamers, hung from what looked to be every reachable place. Finding our name cards on a table, Will and I took our seats.

"Ready for this?" Will asked as the rest of the guests were getting situated. I saw Paddy, West, Rudi, Clinton, and Blue arriving together, and gave a wave. "Promises to be epic. Eight courses."

"I hear it's all about the pacing," I said.

"True … but, as my grandma used to say, we're here for a good time, not for a long time."

"Maybe in this case, both," I said, picking up my chopsticks.

When everyone was seated, Mei began performing a tea ceremony, but it seemed we weren't particularly supposed to pay it any mind as guests at the other tables, as well as our own, began snacking on the hors d'oeuvres and chatting amongst themselves. I told Will about my morning at Mei's and the processional walk to Roger's, and Will agreed that the bridal party was certainly the more active of the two. At Roger's, they pretty much just hung around waiting for us to arrive.

And then, with the tea ceremony apparently over, a bevy of servers descended, bringing with them the expected copious amounts of food: sea cucumber, lobster, a whole fish, a whole chicken, a platter of duck, and two kinds of soup, a spicy one as well as some sort of hot fruit one. Plates of noodles were also placed on each table, in case any of us were in need of a starch to help fill up. When everyone was done eating, platters of watermelon chunks arrived, and Roger and Mei came around to toast each table with bottles of rice wine and 7Up. Then, it was time for the cake cutting and the rolling out of the karaoke machine. A group of us was soon crowded around the microphone, belting out an enthusiastic rendition of "My Heart Will Go On," while, in the center of the room, Mei's parents had started a conga line.

At the end of the evening, when we'd all gathered outside the restaurant to see the happy couple off, someone set off a box of a hundred-shot fireworks, which immediately knocked itself over and sent us all, along with a host of unsuspecting bystanders, scattering behind lampposts, trees, and cars in retreat. Roger and Mei made a dash for their car, and for a few moments, everyone remained where they were, hidden from the artillery, until the fireworks had shot themselves out. Then, seeing that no injuries or damages had been sustained, everyone exploded into laughter. Rolling down their window, Roger made a joke about "getting sent off with a bang," and then, with a wave, they were off.

Back in the apartment, Will and I and the three friends all collapsed onto the living room sofa and chairs, exhausted and fairly drunk.

"We did it," Will said. "Got 'em married."

"Got 'em married," I said, hardly able to keep my eyes open.

One of the friends went into the kitchen and came back with a bottle of tequila and a stack of glasses.

"Time for the after party," he said, holding up the bottle and giving it a jaunty shake.

"Not for me," I said. Arguing that the bridal party had had to make an earlier start to the day, I was, after a few minutes, eventually successful in convincing them to let me go and said my good nights.

"Good night," Will said as I was headed down the hall. "And, hey, we made it through."

"It's all about the pacing," I called back.

Back in the bedroom, with my head spinning as I changed into my pajamas, I tried to take hold of a thought, any thought, to anchor myself to something concrete. *I have been drunk just twice in my life.* The *Gatsby* line popped into my head, and, lying down, I let myself think back over the scene. Poor Nick always seemed so out of his element and yet simultaneously so awkwardly aware. But maybe that's the plight of the narrator, to always be watching yourself, within and without, looking up and wondering how you got to wherever you were and if you belonged there. Closing my eyes, I told myself I didn't have to think of it now. I didn't have to know where things would end up. There'd be time to think after the summer, or after another year, or after another. The sound of celebratory drinking slowly faded into the background.

* * *

With Roger and Mei gone for the week, postponing a proper honeymoon in lieu of touring Beijing with Roger's family, the restaurant was short-staffed, so I offered to help out. I wasn't much of a cook, so while Clinton and Will took care of things in the kitchen, I helped Blue out front, taking orders and ambitiously trying to fill the role of tourist-whisperer. Happily, Paddy, West, and Rudi were sticking around during the week, but otherwise, the end of the semester had begun to bring about a noticeable decline in the attendance of regulars. Both Paul and Jen, as well as a few others I had only previously heard mention of, came by early in the week to say their farewells, their foreign teaching stints having come to an end, and I wondered if any of them would find their way up north, perhaps filling the spot I had recently vacated. It felt a little strange to think of myself in this way, interchangeable and expendable, like nothing more than a chess piece swapping places with others around the board. But, then again, maybe this was the nature of any job, really. Maybe there would always be someone else who could do it. I couldn't decide whether this was a depressing thought or a liberating one, so I convinced myself it could be the latter.

At any rate, it wasn't all farewells. With a hapless, camera-toting stride, the start of the tourist season also kicked off. By my second day in the restaurant, I had had conversations with travelers as varied as their itineraries: a British couple touring some of China's most prominent cities—Beijing, Shanghai, Guangzhou, and here in Kunming; three Dutch girls who, having recently completed a trip across the Tran-Siberian Railway, were now making their way down through China and into Southeast Asia; an American girl having just recently finished an internship working with different methods of artificial insemination in pandas at the breeding center in Chengdu and stopping in Kunming before making her way to a wildlife reserve in Singapore. Some of the people who passed through were the sort with whom I could easily imagine being friends, if ever we had the occasion to interact together regularly; and some were not. But still, for the most part, it was easy to be friendly with anyone for a couple of hours. Plus, I now realized why Will was so full of trivia—it was amazing all the bits of information one could pick up from random conversations with strangers.

"Did you know that the first Americans to see a panda were two of Teddy Roosevelt's sons?" I asked Will as we were cleaning up at the end of the second day. We still had a full house in the apartment as two of the friends, graduate students, apparently had decided to stay on to conduct some sort of market research and/or grant proposal; I remember the term "data collection" being thrown around a lot. At any rate, though they made for a fun group, these quiet evenings with just Will and I closing up the restaurant together were all I wanted—a few, fleeting moments of peace amidst what had otherwise been such a chaotic summer.

"Really? No, that's a new one to me," he said, pausing his scrubbing of the stove top. "So, let's see, that would have been, what? Nineteen … twenties? Early thirties?"

"Spot on. Nineteen twenty-eight." I finished washing out one of the many beer glasses filling the sink and set it upside down on the draining board. "It was while they were on an expedition over here. They saw a panda and promptly shot it. Then they had it stuffed and sent to the Field Museum in Chicago. I guess it's still there, according to this girl who was telling me about it today."

"Sounds about right," he said, rinsing off his sponge. "The American response to the new and unknown: kill it or take it. Or both." He picked up a towel and began drying one of the freshly washed glasses. "Have you seen the pandas? In Chengdu, I mean."

"During the winter holiday, just before I came here."

"Ah, the ill-fated winter holiday."

"Yeah, well, it wasn't all bad," I said.

"Hey, that reminds me." He had been rubbing a spot on the glass he was drying but stopped for a moment. "We still have a little summer left. Why don't we try again for a trip? You can finally use that ticket to Thailand."

"I don't know. Things are just so busy. I can't imagine how the timing's going to work out."

"Oh, come on. You've got a good imagination." He set down his glass and put his hands on the counter on either side of me. As always, though, it was those blue eyes that pinned me to the spot. "Let me book it for Monday. We'll just go for a week. My friends don't need me around, and Roger and Mei will be back by then, plus they've got Clinton and Blue to help with the restaurant. What do you say?"

"That's unfair," I said after he kissed me.

"So, is that a yes?"

And though I knew, of course, he could work it all out and make it happen, you can't blame me for telling him I needed a little more convincing.

* * *

The next day, we got a summer shower that showed signs of lingering longer than usual, and I could tell that the group who was camped out in the loft, composed of a Buddhist Frenchman en route to Tibet, two Austrians doing some Himalayan hiking, and three Danes on a bike trip around Asia, all young men and all smelling distinctly of weed, were planning on hanging out for the duration. Taking a tray full of beers upstairs, I recalled the word that came to mind after my very first night of conversation in the loft back in January, and it seemed just as fitting at this moment: unlikely. Or, at least, an unlikely group for me to be spending an afternoon with. And yet, as Will would say, here we all were.

"I thought it'd be hard to find here," I heard one of the Danes say on my way up the stairs, "but actually, it was quite easy. And cheap. Twenty dollars can buy you enough to smoke until you puke."

"I would still be very careful, though," one of the Austrians warned. "I hear the penalties are very severe and that China is not the place you want to go to prison."

"Just don't get caught smuggling," the Dane continued. "I don't think they'll bother us just for smoking; but smuggling? Probably you are not so lucky." I reached the top of the stairs in time to see him draw a thumb across his neck while making a *qwwk* slashing sound.

"More like this," the Frenchman said as he held up his fingers in the shape of a gun. "I have read that China still executes by firing squad." Seeing me, he asked, "True?"

"Supposedly," I said, handing out the beers. "That, and sometimes by lethal injection, I guess." Once again, I had my students to thank for this information as it had come up during a class debate regarding capital punishment.

"See?" said one of Austrians. "I think we have to be very careful."

"We will all be worm food someday," said one of the other Danes, smiling as he accepted his beer. "We might as well go happy."

The Frenchman took a sip from his glass. "And you think a bullet through the head or life in a Chinese prison is happiness?"

The Dane, obviously unconcerned with either of these prospects being anything more than hypothetical, shrugged.

Having arranged their empties on my tray, I gave a nod to indicate my leaving.

"What do you think?" the unconcerned Dane asked, stopping me before I could make my exit. "What is the happiest way to go?"

"I don't know," I said. "Neither of those options sounds very good to me."

"Better safe than sorry," said one of his Danish compatriots in what sounded like a butchered attempt at a John Wayne accent.

"Something like that." I returned the smile, then turned and headed down the stairs before I could get pulled further into the conversation.

At the bar, I found Will standing, looking over a ledger.

"What's the discussion turned to now?" he asked after finishing a tally.

"Pot," I said. "And I think something about how risky it may or may not be to get in China. I didn't have much to contribute; not really my area of expertise."

"Never let a lack of knowledge get in the way of a good conversation." He looked up from his book and rolled his shoulders in a stretch. "I'm pretty sure that's the backpacker motto, anyway. And it seems to me that the subject is fairly inconsequential. Something about traveling just makes people want to talk … any random topic will usually do."

"Including, apparently, the best ways to die. That's what they were moving on to when I left."

"Ah, death. One thing that unites us all."

Just then we heard a commotion outside, and both of us turned to look out through the window. A typical small red taxi had just pulled up along the sidewalk in front of the restaurant, and in the back, through the half-lowered car door window, we could make out a *waiguoren*, clearly engaged in an argument with the driver.

"Speaking of communication," Will said, "looks like this guy could use a little help with it."

He headed outside as I stood watching from the doorway. I could see that the argument was heated, but from what I could tell, neither party was making much headway. With shouts coming in English from one side and Mandarin from the other, it seemed more of a yelling match than anything else.

"Can I help?" Will asked just as the back door of the car flung open.

The passenger, a guy around our age with close-cropped blond hair, wearing a sleeveless t-shirt and aggressive expression, stepped out of the car with a snort.

"Doubt it," he said. "This jackass is just trying to rip me off. I told him to take me to The Foreign Party, and he nods like he knows it, but then he brings me here."

When Will didn't immediately answer, the guy looked

annoyed and added, "It's supposed to be a cool bar around here."

"Well, this is The Foreign Burrito," Will said. "Of course, I'm biased, but I think it's a pretty cool bar, too. And, though I'm pretty sure I know most of the bars in the city, I've never heard one by that name."

"Foreign Party, Foreign Parties, something like that. A backpacker I met in Guangzhou told me about it. They have, like, different parts of the bar decorated with stuff from different countries and serve weird drinks from around the world or something." His voice was loud with frustration. It seemed to me that he could have come straight from boot camp. All he was missing were the dog tags.

"Oh, right," Will said, suddenly making the connection. "Global Parties. I totally forgot about that place. But, yeah, it's kinda cool."

Will was being generous, I knew. Global Parties was a running joke among expats in Kunming, and after Will took me there once to experience the overpriced beer and perpetual spring break anything-goes atmosphere for myself, I could see why. But perhaps that was what this guy was looking for. He actually seemed like the kind of guy who might enjoy it.

"It's on the other side of town, though," Will continued. "Where exactly did you ask him to take you?"

"I don't know. I had the chick working at the hostel write it out in Chinese for me. I asked her if she knew about this bar called The Foreign Party—that's what the dude in Guangzhou called it—and she said yes and wrote it down for me to show to a taxi driver." He held up a small strip of paper. "So, I go out and show it to this fuckwit, and he nods like he knows where it is, but then he brings me here." He gave a gloomy look toward the restaurant.

Will asked to see the paper, and the guy handed it to him.

"Right," Will said after taking a look. "Well, to be fair, I'm sure it was an honest misunderstanding." I could see that Will didn't want to throw the woman at the hostel under the bus any more than he wanted to place blame on anyone present, so he said, "Foreign Party, Foreign Burrito, you can see the mix-up."

"Well, I'll be fucked if I'm paying him for it. I have to go all the way back in the opposite direction now."

The rain had begun to pick up again, so Will said, "Why don't you come inside for a minute. I'll write you out directions to the other place, and we'll get you all sorted. A beer on the house."

The guy shrugged but decided to take him up on the offer, turning to come inside. Will said something to the driver, and I saw him hand him a few *renminbi* bills. Apparently satisfied, the taxi sped off.

Jimmy, as we learned he was called after we introduced ourselves, decided this place looked "okay enough" to have a drink or two and ended up staying a couple of hours in the loft with the others. The dinner crowd soon picked up, so I saw little of him until he came downstairs as he was getting ready to leave. He was chatting with Will at the bar when I overheard him say that he, too, would be flying down to Bangkok in a few days.

"Maybe we'll see you there," Will said as he gave Jimmy the new directions that he had written down. Then he headed outside with him to flag down another taxi.

I knew he was just being nice, but, thankfully, I thought as I grabbed two menus and went to greet a couple who had just walked in, seeing this guy again seemed pretty unlikely.

* * *

"Definitely," Roger said when he and Mei returned at the end of the week and heard about our plan for going to Thailand. "After two weeks with our families, trust me, getting back to the restaurant will feel like a vacation for us. Go, have fun."

Nevertheless, as we closed up on our final evening before flying out, I found that I was in no hurry to leave.

"You alright?" Will asked, evidently seeing something in my expression as he came down from the loft. I was standing at the bar, having finished in the kitchen and was now doing nothing in particular.

"Just enjoying what will likely be the last evening of calm in Kunming for a while. When we get back, there will be lesson planning and new people arriving and a new schedule to learn—basically, it'll be the start of a whole new year."

He stepped close and reached up into a cupboard behind me to pull down his Red Sox cap and our things.

"Stay just like that," I said, putting my hands on his chest. "I want to remember the quiet before it's over."

He raised an eyebrow and smiled. "You have a funny idea of quiet. It's been nothing but insanity all summer. Actually, I think next year's going to be perfect. Plus, we have Thailand. All kinds of quiet ahead." But still, he stayed another minute before handing me my bag and adjusting his hat on his head. He gave a glance around the room then gave a nod toward the door.

I stepped outside and watched as he set the alarm, closed the door, and locked down the shutter.

"Okay, then. One last late-night summer dinner? Soak in the city?" he asked.

I nodded.

"White Steps or Broken Fish Tank?"

White Steps, Broken Fish Tank, foreigner, teacher—when you were a *waiguoren*, I had learned, you lived in a world not of names but of descriptions.

"White Steps," I said. "They've got the best dry-fried green beans."

We walked quietly for a while down the sidewalk, allowing the noises and sights of the city to wash over us. Kunming, I had noticed, was a city that displayed its evenings well: the streets pulsed in a blur of colors; skyscrapers bathed in high-beam white light; glowing red neon Chinese characters soared twenty stories above; an ad for Coke quickly followed by one for Samsung played on the jumbotron running around a corner of the mall. And even at this late hour, people were out, some strolling arm in arm along the pedestrian street, others seated on benches or at outdoor tables set up by adjoining restaurants. What I liked best, though, were the things so different from home: the dragon sculptures lining the sidewalk; the ancient city gates, now serving as roundabouts in the middle of a busy road; the red lanterns swaying overhead; and the night market stalls with their wares of brightly-colored bags, traditional-style jewelry, and cheap t-shirts, all illuminated by a single exposed light bulb, the cords for which lay knotted underfoot. In a blend of time and place, it was all here—even the waning outlines of the mountains could be made out in the distance—and it wasn't hard to see why this was a place where one might choose to stay.

"I know I asked you this once before, but, really, do you imagine yourself staying here indefinitely?" I asked the question abruptly, almost as if the stream of consciousness in my head had suddenly developed a voice.

"It's funny," Will said as we turned down a side street toward the restaurant. "When I first moved here, I was so focused on getting the business up and running that I didn't really give much thought to anything past the start-up phase. It was all just one small step after another, and I don't know if either Roger or I ever really expected it to work out. But now that it has, it feels like it just kind of snuck up on me. One day I looked around and realized this was home."

"So, you do? You feel at home here?"

Will thought a moment.

"Well, there will always be things that remind me of my *waiguoren* status—I'll always have to show my passport and, as you know, can't go more than a few minutes walking down the sidewalk without being stared and shouted at—but, yeah, I would say I feel as at home here as anywhere."

I knew Will's family situation was different, but, for me, it was a hard idea to get used to, that choosing to live here didn't somehow mean a rejection of life back home.

"And Rog, it seems, is in for the long haul. So, there's that," he added. Having reached the restaurant, which was indeed accessed by three white steps, he held open the door, and we went inside.

It was an old building, a single shabby room, and we chose a table away from the corner where a group of young workmen were playing a loud drinking game. I had seen this game before, something involving short, sharp fist pounds on the table that knocked out a beat in accompaniment to a series of counted numbers: *Yi! Er! San! Si! Wu! Liu!*—a Chinese workmen equivalent to Paper, Rock, Scissors, it seemed. The place was noisy and smoke-filled, but the food was worth it.

"I do like it here, though," Will said after we had taken our seats and placed our order. He took off his hat and set it to one side of the table, then brushed a hand through his hair.

"In Kunming, I mean. There'd be a lot of things I'd miss about it if I were to leave. Of course, there are things I miss about Boston, too. Baseball, for one: summer nights at the ballpark, watching the Sox. And the Pats, too; lounging on the couch, watching Sunday afternoon football." He paused as he poured us each a cup of tea. "People, too; but, you know, mostly sports."

He smiled as the *fuwuyuan* arrived with the food, prompt as always, and we both took a moment to scoop a few chopsticks full of egg and tomatoes and spicy green beans onto our respective bowls of rice.

"What about you?" he asked after a few bites.

"What do I miss about home, or do I think I could stay in Kunming indefinitely?"

"Either. Both."

I laid my chopsticks against the edge of my bowl and picked up my small, handle-less ceramic teacup.

"I think sometimes I miss just feeling normal, being able to blend in." I took a sip, then gave the cup a couple of swirls and watched as the loose bits of leaves floated to the top and sunk again. "And I miss my family, being a part of their lives—birthday parties, Sunday dinners, Christmas, and all that. Seahawks' games too, of course."

Will shook his head. "You can't help that—it's just the way you were raised."

I made a face, then continued.

"But at the same time, I know I can't just stay there, expecting everything to remain the same as it's always been. People move, family dynamics change, what we want from life …" I picked up my chopsticks again and pinched a green bean. "Anyway, I can see what you mean when you say that things just kind of happen."

"Yeah, but …"

We were interrupted by the loud sound of scraping chairs, which drew our attention over toward the group of workmen. As they stood up from the table, a pushing match broke out among a few of them, and they practically climbed over one another in their attempts to be the first at the counter to pay for the group. If I hadn't known better, I would have thought it was a serious fight instead of the show of respect that it was.

"Yeah, but what?" I asked, wanting to hear what he was going to say.

"Anne." He stopped and looked at me.

"What?" I said. Then, after a moment, more nervously, "What?"

He smiled. "Nothing. I just think … well, first of all, I think home is where we make it. But, secondly, I don't believe for one second that you're just going to let your life happen to you. I've never met a person who thinks as carefully over each decision and implication as you do. To be honest, I admire it. It makes me wonder if I should think a little bit more about what I'm doing."

"No," I said. "I like how you can respond so easily, in the moment, to anything. I wish I could get out of my own head."

"Well, then," he said, "that's why we're a good team. You help me think through things a little more, and I help you …"

"Think a little less?"

"I was going to say, 'live in the moment,'" he said, grinning as he watched the last of the workmen leaving. "But, yes, we'll help each other find balance."

CHAPTER ELEVEN

~ Falling Back ~

By the afternoon of our second day in Bangkok, I had already managed to accomplish quite a few firsts. I had taken a water taxi to see a floating market of boats piled high with sweet-smelling, alien-looking fruits. I had been compelled to rent pants to wear over my shorts in order to visit the Grand Palace and see a giant reclining Buddha. I had drunk cold sweetened condensed milk coffee from a plastic bag tied off with a rubber band at the top, packaged like a goldfish won at the county fair. And now, with the evening yet to be filled before heading off in the morning by bus to a beach town three hours south of the city, Will said we might as well take advantage of one more first the city had to offer.

"Thai boxing: Thailand's most popular sport." He almost looked like some kind of street poet, reciting the line off an advertising poster plastered to a light pole we were passing.

"It says it's a cultural experience not to be missed. Might be good for your book."

"Well, there you have it," I said. "It's a sign. Literally."

Back at our hostel, we mentioned our plans to the young Thai guy manning the reception desk and asked if he had any recommendations of places where we could go see it. He nodded as though he had been expecting this question all along.

"Of course. Today is Tuesday, so … here."

He took a flyer from a stack piled on a table behind him and held it out to us between long slender fingers.

"Lumpinee Boxing Stadium. Fights every Tuesday, Friday, and Saturday at 6:00 p.m. Other nights, different place; but tonight, you go here. You want? I arrange tickets for you. Ringside."

"Sure," I said, briefly looking over the pamphlet. "I don't think we need ringside, though. I think this middle tier looks fine."

Will, resting his chin on my shoulder, took a quick look and agreed.

Our host looked hesitant a moment.

"Most foreigners sit ringside …" He looked as though he were waiting for us to reconsider, but when we didn't, he nodded and continued, "I think you are right. It is not necessary. Third tier is not good—only for standing and gambling—but second tier, I think it is okay. Tonight, you will be like Thai people."

"Another first," I said.

* * *

After an early dinner, we arrived at the stadium via *tuk-tuk*, a sort of motorized rickshaw, and were thrown into the hustle and flow of spectators, food carts, and souvenir hawkers. It was a large arena, and other than the fact that the surrounding streets were lined with motorcycles instead of cars, it didn't feel that different from any large sporting event back home.

"You finally get your wish," I shouted to Will as we began following a crowd toward one of several entrances. "Sports."

"Should have brought my foam finger," Will yelled back, holding up his ticket with one hand and holding on to me with the other as we passed inside.

The arena, fanning up and away from the ring at the center, was already holding a few thousand people, by the looks of it, and continued to fill with a steady stream of onlookers.

"Wow, the sign wasn't lying," I said, still loudly, preparing to show our tickets again to a man in an orange security vest. "Popular, indeed."

We were pointed toward our section, which was behind a low wire fence, separating us from the ringside section in front, and we found seats on a wooden bench a few rows from the divider. True to our hostel receptionist's description, the third-tier section behind us was really just a platform. There were no seats, and the people there had their backs to us and were shouting and making frantic gestures, similar to what one might see at the floor of the New York Stock Exchange. Apparently, the betting had begun.

"This isn't bad at all," Will said, looking down toward the ring over the fifteen or so rows of metal folding chairs in front of us. "Although, ringside is awfully close, isn't it?"

"But remember, this is more authentic."

"That's right. Tonight, we are like Thai people."

Spectators were still filing in when suddenly the noise level inside the arena kicked up a notch, and I looked toward the ring to discover the reason: two fighters, one in red, the other in blue, were making their entrance. They strolled up to the ring and, after ducking under the ropes, bounced around for about a minute until they stopped and, with a series of kneels and bows, performed what looked to be some sort of prayer or ceremony. Then they disrobed quickly and stood bare-chested, facing each other, waiting to begin.

An accompaniment of clashing sounds and horn-type music erupted almost simultaneously with the sound of the starting bell, and I scanned the auditorium in search of its source. I soon found it, off to one side of the ring, in the form of a small band consisting of a clarinet, two snare drums, a pair of cymbals, and a large gong. Both in look and sound, they seemed something of a cross between a group of snake charmers and a marching band.

"Impressively loud for just five people," I said to Will, cupping one hand around my mouth and using my other to point them out.

"Yeah, loud," he said, nodding. "Thai pep band."

For the first minute or so, the two fighters—who I soon realized were probably just teenagers—didn't do much in the way of fighting. Instead, they each faced the other and began tapping a foot out in front of themselves, like a couple of adolescent bulls sizing each other up before making a charge. Then, just as I began wondering how long they might keep this up, the fighter in red sprung up with a roundhouse kick aimed directly at his opponent's head. In response, the blue fighter, in a motion that looked almost as though he were combing his hair from front to back, positioned his bicep and forearm beside his ear to absorb the blow. The cymbals clashed together, and the crowd cheered. The fighters then rushed toward each other and wrapped their arms around one another's neck. Now locked in a clinch, their only available move seemed to be repeated knee lifts into the other's ribs, and they performed this back and forth several times, nearly in sync with the beat knocked out by the drum player. After several seconds, the blue fighter finally broke free with a jerking motion of both arms. His attempt to follow with an uppercut, though, was less successful as the red fighter ducked to one side. Then, grabbing his opponent's arm and giving it a twist, the red fighter suddenly flipped the blue to the ground. The crowd and band responded instantly, and the blue fighter scrambled to his feet. Soon the two fighters were squaring off again. Just as another bout of bull-like foot-tapping began, the bell sounded, and the round was finished.

The next few rounds were much the same, with the fighters executing a variety of moves and the band and crowd answering by way of loud clashes, bangs, oohs and aahs. In the fifth and final round, the red fighter, pushing out of a hold with a flail of his elbow, caught the blue fighter just above the eye and opened up a nasty cut. A stream of blood began rushing down the injured fighter's face, and from the way he was blinking and swiping at it, I wondered if he could even see. Luckily for him, the final bell soon sounded, and the fight was over.

The judges made a quick tally of points, and within moments, the verdict was delivered: the referee lifted the red fighter's glove in victory. The crowd applauded, but it seemed to me that people's interest had already moved on to the next fight. The fighters in the ring seemed to understand this as well, for after a couple of quick bows to each other and to the crowd, both ducked under the ropes and were gone. The band, too, instantly went quiet. Clearly, it was break time.

"Lively," Will said as we followed the lead of those around us and stood to stretch our legs. "So, one fight down, seven to go. We certainly get our money's worth, don't we?

"Hey," he interjected abruptly. He nodded toward the front of the crowd. "Isn't that the guy who showed up at the restaurant last week after the taxi mix-up? The one looking for the bar?"

I followed the direction of Will's gaze and spotted the guy he was referring to just as the guy spotted us in return.

So much for it being unlikely, I thought as I watched Jimmy make his way up the stairs and into our section, jostling against people heading in the opposite direction, presumably in search of refreshments, toilets, or bet-making.

"Jesus!" he said when he got to our row. He pushed back against a man who was trying to make his way past, and the man gave him an unhappy look before moving on.

"Why the fuck are you guys all the way back here?" he asked when he finally reached us.

"Well, you know, when in Rome," Will said. "Talk about a small world, though, huh? How's Thailand treating you so far?"

After describing a few bars and his hostel, as well as offering his opinion on Thai women and proclaiming Thailand to be "a hundred times better than China," Jimmy nodded toward the ring and added, "These guys are pretty wimpy-looking, though, aren't they? I thought it was going to be more like MMA-style, cage-fighting type stuff since supposedly it was created by the Thai military to train their soldiers in hand-to-hand combat. But if this is the best they've got, maybe we ought to think about invading. Wouldn't be too hard to take these guys down."

"I don't know," Will said. "I'm pretty sure they could take me. Elbow to the eye—that'd be me done."

I leaned in against Will's back, as he was, thankfully, between Jimmy and me. This seemed the smallest effort I could make to be part of the conversation while saying nothing.

"Yeah, right," Jimmy said, as though responding to a joke. "Anyway, I'm going to go place some bets and see if that helps make it a little more interesting."

With the music starting up again, he began making his way back down the row. "I'll come find you again after the next fight," he promised before turning to head up the stairs.

Will gave a wave.

"Funny running into him here, isn't it?" he said, turning to me.

"Yeah," I said. "Funny."

Will smiled. "Oh, come on, he's probably not so bad. Most likely, just a little lonely."

"My good opinion once lost," I said, returning the smile. But I liked that Will was naturally inclined to give others the benefit of the doubt, so I added, "But I'll try to be nice."

"You are nice," Will said, tapping my chin with his knuckle, Humphrey Bogart style.

I nudged his chest with my forehead. "If you say so."

True to his word, at the conclusion of the second match, which ended in a draw, Jimmy returned. He looked as glum as ever.

"Lose money on the fight?" Will asked.

"No. I went back there, but I couldn't really figure it out. It was just a bunch of guys yelling and making retarded hand signals."

I tried looking somewhat sympathetic, but I was honestly relieved. Thinking back to his encounter with the taxi driver, I could easily imagine any gambling venture of Jimmy's eventually leading to an argument and Will feeling obliged to step in and help mitigate. And my gut told me that the more we could avoid getting caught in the middle of anything with this guy, the better.

"I don't really care," Jimmy continued, shrugging and

trying hard to look as though he meant it. "They probably would have just ripped me off, anyway."

Once again, when the music started back up, Jimmy returned to his seat, having to stop first at a gap in the wire divider to shows his ticket to a security guard before being allowed to pass back into the ringside seating section.

"I wonder if he's going to come back after every fight," I said as another pre-match ceremony got underway inside the ring.

"Well, he is here by himself."

"And you're going to invite him out afterwards." There was no need to ask this as a question. I knew Will, and the kind of unspoken expat code he lived by.

"Feels like it'd be rude not to, right?"

"I know," I said. "It's fine. I'll mentally prepare myself."

The bell rang for the start of the next match.

"And, hey, with any luck, maybe these next fights will get a little more violent. Then we might actually see him happy."

And, of course, having joked about it, I felt a pang of guilt when the third fight did, in fact, turn out to be more gruesome. With one sweeping kick to the leg from the orange-clad fighter, the green fighter went down, crumpling to the mat in what looked to be excruciating pain. He writhed around for a long moment, clutching his leg just below the knee and moaning until a stretcher came and carried him out of the ring. The crowd, perhaps feeling as I did—like an accessory to what had just happened—sat subdued. Jimmy, though, having again made his way back to us, radiated energy.

"Man, did you hear that snap from back here? He went down right in front of me. I bet he broke his leg."

The rest of the evening went much the same: a fight followed by Jimmy coming back to give us his unsolicited commentary. After the next three matches went the full five rounds for two decisions and a draw (all dull, according to Jimmy), we got a knock-out (finally), and, lastly, an unstoppable nosebleed resulting in a TKO.

"I wish they had let that last fight continue," he said predictably when he came back and we all three began making our way out of the stadium. "But I bet if I could figure out how the gambling works, I could make some money at it. I picked the winners every time."

"Well, there you go," I said. "Maybe you should stay in Bangkok a while, see how long you can live off your winnings."

"It's so cheap here, I bet I could. But I kind of want to make it down to the beaches. Where are you guys headed next?"

And though, perhaps due to what is both an art and defense mechanism developed especially by women, I would have answered vaguely or said something along the lines of having not yet decided, Will simply couldn't help himself. He was honest and conversational to a fault.

* * *

At the bus depot the next morning, I took a few steps away from Will and Jimmy and, under the guise of watching for our bus, tried to distract myself by taking in our surroundings. I realized that, other than in the proximity of Jimmy, the atmosphere around the parking lot was quite relaxed, more so than the stations I had been to in China. Here, no one seemed to be in any particular hurry. Crowds formed and disbanded with the arrival and departure of each bus, but with none of the sudden urgency that so permeated life in China. In China, it seemed, you waited until, in an instant, you didn't—from waiting to pushing, or being pushed, then, quickly, waiting again. But here, whether it was due to ambivalence, calm, or simply the sweltering heat mixed with the bus exhaust and tarmac fumes, people just seemed to saunter, onto and off of the bus, into and out of the station, all around the lot. The general feeling seemed to be: We'll get there when, or if, we get there—what's the rush?

After a while, a bus displaying our number lumbered up through the lot and eventually came to rest in the bay in front of us. The doors opened, and a single-file line of passengers trickled out. When the last passenger, an elderly woman, at last succeeded in making her way off the bus, two men followed—one being the driver, and, remembering the shouting teenager on the bus out of Lhasa, I guessed the other to be the ticket taker. Neither of them was wearing any sort of uniform, but there was no mistaking it: they were the ones in charge. While those of us waiting to board looked on, the two men lit up their cigarettes, stretched, then locked up the bus and disappeared into the terminal. It felt a bit odd, not being swept up in a unified crush headed for the waiting door, so perhaps I had acclimated to life in China more than I had realized.

"Yeah, no rush, guys; you're only like twenty minutes late already. But, by all means, take your time," Jimmy said toward the terminal, though with no real threat of being heard, much less understood, by either of the men. The other passengers seemed completely unfazed.

It must be exhausting, I thought to myself, to be as constantly disgusted by the world as Jimmy seemed to be.

"I might as well take a piss, if we're just going to be sitting here for who knows how much longer," Jimmy said. "Watch my bag."

Will and I both nodded as he headed off in search of a toilet.

"I'm sorry," Will said as soon as Jimmy was out of earshot.

If I had tried, I probably could have said something about how Will and I had met just as randomly and that I didn't really want him to be sorry for a personality trait that I and everybody else loved about him. But, as it was, I was too tired to try and too unpracticed in navigating such feelings with Will.

"It's fine," I said, continuing to look out over the tarmac at the waiting crowds. I realized that, for the first time, I didn't really feel like talking to Will. Instead, I wished Kelly or my sister were here. It seemed like they would understand whatever it was I was having trouble articulating.

"Or, it's annoying," Will said, trying to catch my eye. "And it's pretty much my fault."

"It's not your fault," I said, finally meeting his eyes.

He didn't look like he totally believed me, but he waited for me to continue.

"Yes, I'm annoyed. But it is what it is." I paused a moment, checking behind me, and then admitted, "I just can't stand this guy."

"I know," he said. "And for the record, I don't want to be stuck with him for the rest of the trip, either. I just don't know what to do about it."

"You always know what to do," I said, and then immediately regretted it. It sounded like an accusation. "Anyway," I said, softening my tone and giving his arm a squeeze, "you were just being nice. And who knows, maybe he'll want to do his own thing once we get there."

Just then, we both caught sight of Jimmy as he reemerged from the bathroom, his cropped blond head bobbing jerkily above the crowd as he shoved through people on his way back to us. I had a sudden urge to be able to speak Thai, to apologize to everyone around us, or better yet, to explain, *Actually, it's a long story, but he's not really with us.*

"And, hey, there are worse things than being too nice," I said, giving Will's arm another squeeze.

Looking unconvinced, he gave a final nod as he said, "We'll see how it goes."

"Man," Jimmy said before he had even reached us, "just when you think the bathrooms in Asia can't get any worse. It'll be a miracle if I don't catch some horrible disease over here."

With no further opportunity to continue on with our discussion, Will and I stood listening to Jimmy's random travel observations and complaints of it being "hot as balls" for another ten minutes or so before the two men in charge of the bus reappeared. Making their way to the side of the bus, they lifted up the two large cargo doors running along the bottom, and only then did the group around us begin to move, sliding suitcases, duffle bags, boxes, and crates of all description into the underbelly of the bus. Will, Jimmy, and I followed suit, sliding in our backpacks, then making our way onto the bus and into our seats.

Within a few minutes, with everything loaded, the bus started up, and immediately the TV screen at the front flickered to life, picking up in the middle of what looked to be some type of Thai comedy variety show. It was loud, too loud to comfortably talk over, and, after watching for a moment, Will signaled to me that he was putting his headphones in. I nodded and pulled mine out of my pocket, as well. I assumed that Jimmy, sitting behind us, would most likely do the same. It was only a few-hour ride to the beach at Hua Hin, so, turning toward the window, I closed my eyes and tried to imagine how nice the sea air would be. The thought would be better than my typical overthinking, especially since I had that uncomfortable feeling of something being left unresolved, like I was in the middle of an argument but without knowing exactly with whom or over what.

Will's hand was soon on my shoulder, gently shaking me awake.

"Mm hm?" I said, turning toward him, eyes still closed.

"Hey, we're here."

I opened my eyes and saw, past Will, Jimmy stepping into the aisle.

Focusing my gaze back on Will, I spoke aloud the conclusion I had come to before falling asleep. "Let's not do anything, okay?"

"Fuck yeah," Jimmy said. "Just beach, booze, and babes."

Will gave me a half smile. "We'll see," he said.

* * *

"Okay," Will said after we had changed into our beach attire and stepped out of the backdoor of our bungalow and onto the sand. "Good things only for the rest of the afternoon. Clear skies, blue water, the beach at our doorsteps …"

"And crazy cheap," Jimmy added, having learned that our bungalow rentals cost only a dollar per day. "Forget Bangkok. I'm moving here."

The fact that Jimmy had found nothing to complain about and that Will looked ready to relax was good enough for me, but I did have one more thing to add.

"Space," I said, holding my arms out wide. "You forget what a difference it makes." The fact that Jimmy had been given a room a good four huts down from ours had also helped contribute to my mood.

"Shall we?" Will asked, slinging his towel over his shoulder and motioning toward the water.

Just then, a group of beachgoers sprinted by us, their footsteps pounding loudly on the sand. A frisbee came sailing after them.

"Open game," somebody called out in an American accent. "We need numbers."

And just like that, Jimmy was off.

"See ya later," Will called out after him. Then, turning to me, he added, "Wow, that was easy."

"You don't need to find a way to ditch him," I said, moving us down the beach. "This is good enough."

He nodded, but I couldn't shake some residual feeling.

"You shouldn't feel like you have to fix everything. I'm sorry." I looked down the beach and added, "I don't care about Jimmy. I just want us to be okay … and I definitely don't want to be in a fight."

Will stopped walking and looked at me. "We're fine," he said. "Come on. Good vibes only." He laid our towels down on the sand and pulled me down with him. Probably still sensing my hesitation, he continued, "If that was a fight, we've got to learn to do it better. First of all, you're doing way too much thinking again."

"That's right, you were going to teach me to think less, remember?"

"I believe that was to 'live in the moment,'" he said, kicking sand on my foot. "But, yes, sometimes thinking less is also good." With that, he laid back and closed his eyes, his face and chest lit up from the brightness of the sun. I turned over on my side and, placing my hand on his chest, watched it rise and fall with his breathing, learning to balance.

* * *

And this is how we spent those days: lost in the respite of the beach, undiminished by the presence of others. We did, in fact, end up doing many things in a group—usually joining with the two Irish guys and the French couple staying in the neighboring bungalows—but this only helped in diffusing any one particular person's point of view. Plus, with no agenda and no other place we needed to be, it was easy to fall into a kind of routine that none of us, including Jimmy, could find much to be annoyed about. Each morning we slept late, lulled by the sound of the waves lapping just beneath our window, and then spent all day on the beach, feeling the sun on our faces and the heat from the sand seeping up through our towels as we read, napped, and chatted. When we were hot, we went for dips in the water; when we were hungry and thirsty, we bought mangoes and chilled Cokes from the children who carried them on trays and waited for us as we drank, ready to collect the empty glass bottles for return. Will and I had fallen into a comfortable rhythm in this overall daytime tranquility, and, for my part, I was even able to somewhat quiet my mind, finding it natural to occupy myself as a spectator to the activities happening around us: tourists paying to ride horses up and down the beach, overly-tanned retirees walking along hand in hand, topless women and Speedo-clad men strolling up from the water to sunbathe on their towels. Nothing, for a change, seemed pressing, and, though never good at being carefree, my thoughts could at least drift more easily. Not even Jimmy riding by on a horse, making immature gestures, or shaking out his towel too close, flipping sand into my eyes, bothered me as much as it could have. He was just like any other traveler, I decided; we just happened to be going the same way for the same brief moment in time.

And, as pleasant as the days were, the evenings were fun. With the sun beginning to dip behind the horizon, we would pack up, leave the beach, and return to our rooms for a shower and change into fresh clothes before setting off again to dinner, feeling cool and clean, rested, and ready to rejoin the large, rowdy group for a night on the town.

The town was small, comprised of one main street made almost entirely of bars and restaurants, but it demanded one's full attention, from every angle. As we walked along, a chorus of receptionists called out to us in loud, friendly voices, "Best Italian. Fresh seafood. Local curries. Have a look, please. Very cheap." They were all specials, they said, especially for us. Each night we chose whichever menu caught our eye, based on the smallest factor, and, after eating, it was off to the bars. White-haired men with various European and American accents and sun-dried, leathery skin invited us to join them at darts and pool and would ring the bell for another round whenever the mood grew particularly festive. Sometimes one of them left early, his hand on a young Thai woman's shoulder and a grin on his face as his friends called out to him and rang the bell for another, but when we left, there was no such fuss. The old men merely lifted their drinks and sent us off with a "Take care, kids."

On the way back toward our rooms, we'd make a group 7-11 stop for a few more beers and then sit outside in chairs on the deck or the nearby pier, playing cards and drinking until the early hours when it was finally time to call it a night, return to bed, and, once again, fall into easy rhythm to the sound of the waves.

We spent three days like this, uncomplicated and happy, and when we left, it was only because we wanted to see more. After saying our goodbyes to the Irish and the French, we boarded another bus, this time heading nine hours south along the Thai-Burmese border until eventually crossing a bridge onto the island of Phuket. And, by now, I hardly thought twice about Jimmy joining us—wherever I went and whatever the circumstances, as long as Will was coming, too, I believed peace would always follow.

* * *

Squeezed into a *tuk-tuk* on our way from the bus terminal to the center of town, I felt like a pilot coming in on arrival. Not only was our small, motorized carriage about the size of a cramped jet cockpit, but the road itself, with its row of streetlights on either side, gave its best impression of an oceanside runway. Evenly spaced palm trees and a sidewalk helped mark the separation between street and beach on one side, and on the other a steady stream of adrenaline-pumping shops and restaurants advertised with neon signs: a glowing red PIZZA COMPANY, a towering pair of golden arches, a giant green shamrock and spotlight shining on a Molly Malone's, the word COFFEE in blinding white. It was like a sort of drug, this constant bombardment of stimuli. BAR AND GRILL. GOGO BAR. WORLD FAMOUS. BEER GARDEN. TIGER. THAI MASSAGE. DISCO! LOVE SHACK. OPEN. WELCOME. COCKTAILS. LADYBOYS. LIVE SHOWS. A pancake street cart strung with Christmas lights sat along the side of the road while vendors selling newspapers, DVDs, and trinkets shone lights on their dizzying selection. Seated outside at tables with giant collapsed umbrellas sticking out from their centers, tourists sat facing the street, looking toward the beach as a row of red *tuk-tuks* awaited their finish, ready to take them wherever next they wanted to go.

By the time we arrived at our hostel and were ushered back into dorm life amidst a barrage of thumping music, it was clear that our laid-back beachside bungalow days were behind us. Here, everything was built on energy, energy manifested in an almost desperate need for excitement, and there seemed to be an unspoken agreement regarding participation. This was a collective objective. Those who wanted quiet, private, or calm, apparently, could go elsewhere.

Jimmy, of course, was right in his element. After half an hour and a few mai tais into our first evening out, that much was obvious. In this world, a place where one drink could easily turn into ten and louder equaled better, he was the poster boy. And since Will naturally fit in anywhere, this only left the question of me. As soon as we had arrived here, I had told myself this wasn't what I liked, what I wanted, or what I needed before heading into another year of unknowns. To me, this place was instantly recognizable as shallow, pointless, and a frivolous outlet for thoughtless people. But as the evening raced on and we bounced around from sticky shot-glass-strewn tiki bar to pulsating club to one of any in-between greasy fried chicken windows, I found myself thinking of Tibet, the mountain, the look by the cliff's edge, and I began to consider that perhaps there was a point, after all; perhaps an embrace of the shallow was, in its own way, a response to the dangers of depth. Here, in the shallow, everything about our subconscious, most ethereal selves seemed to become incarnate. Our desires and fears, our dreams and frustrations, our vitality and encumbrances—this is where they became real, living, flesh. With a moving, breathing, sweating urgency, people were finding something: if not peace, then at least a sort of freedom among the chaos, and I envied them, willing myself to join in the letting go, in the thinking less.

"Are you okay?" Will shouted as we stood at the bar, refreshing our drinks after an indeterminate amount of time on the dance floor. "It's a million degrees in here."

Nodding, I drank down my gin and tonic in thirsty gulps. "Hot as balls?" I asked.

He laughed. "Something like that." He set down his beer and ordered us two waters. "You know we're going to feel this in the morning."

I nodded again and, over the top of Beyoncé singing about

how she was looking so crazy, said, "But I think I don't care."

* * *

The next morning, I awoke early—or at half past nine, what was sure to be much earlier than anyone else—and dressed quietly, not wanting to disturb Will or Jimmy or any of the other three people still asleep in the six-bunk room. Tearing a page from my notebook, I wrote, "Back around noon," and placed it on my bed before slipping out. I was ready to give Patong Beach, now in the light of day, another blurry-eyed look.

With no destination in mind, I set out down the sidewalk and, per my usual wandering habit, turned down whichever road looked of interest. In stark contrast to the previous night, the place was dead. In fact, it reminded me quite a lot of Yinchuan at midday: shops closed and people asleep, an intermission between the acts. As I walked, though, I saw the first signs of a return to life: a storefront reopening, a restaurant worker beginning to set out stools on which, I supposed, customers could eat their breakfast, at whatever time that may be. Even the alley dogs stretched and yawned before sauntering over to begin sniffing their way around corner dumpsters. Outside of one of the shops, a teenage boy was arranging brightly colored mopeds into two rows.

Seeing me, he smiled and asked, in English, "Moto? You want?"

I hesitated. I had seen people driving these around—mopeds with a push-button ignition and a platform on which to put one's feet, groceries, or, in some cases, children—but I had never driven one, not like this.

"Do you have one like this?" I asked, making a motion as though sitting astride a motorcycle, kicking it to life. "Kick start?"

Surprisingly, the boy nodded and directed me to follow him around to the back of the shop.

"Much faster," he said, pointing at the one lonely-looking motorcycle before us. The metal gas tank was covered in scratches, and there was a bit of foam, browned from exposure, flowering out of a large tear in the back of the seat, but otherwise it looked much like the motorcycles I grew up riding around my family's farm.

"Yes, much faster. And more fun." I smiled. "How much?"

After settling on a price, I made no hesitation. I paid for two days.

Surrounded by pedestrians who were now starting to populate the side roads, I drove cautiously at first. But when I got back onto the main road, I twisted down on the throttle and was instantly transported to the wooded trails and creekside paths where my siblings and I grew up riding, trying to lose each other around turns and seeing who could get the most air flying over hills. Here, the worn-out shocks meant I felt every bump, but still, when I leaned low over the handlebars, swerving to avoid potholes and rocks, the bike responded like any other, controlled with the slightest shift of weight, here to the left, there to the right, no need to overdirect, no time to overthink, just … reacting. Naturally, the balance took care of itself.

I could have driven for hours, straight up the ocean road, free to see where it took me, without a thought of anything, except … after about thirty minutes, I found myself turning back.

Pulling up in front of our hostel, I saw that Will was just then sitting down to coffee in the open-air patio.

"Hey, early bird," he said as I flipped down the kickstand. "You have a biker gang meeting this morning or what?"

I smoothed out my windblown hair and shirt as I walked up the patio steps and, saying nothing, kissed him. A long, assured kiss.

"Wow, someone's in a good mood," he said, smiling, as I took the seat opposite him.

"I *am* in a good mood," I said. "Today's going to be a good day."

We ordered breakfast, and Will asked if I had something particular in mind.

"How about one of these?" I offered, pulling out a brochure of motorbike routes I had picked up at the rental shop.

I pushed the map into the center of the table and traced a gold-colored loop with my finger, then held it there as I read the description.

"This one's called the Golden Monkey Way. 'Perfect for those wanting to explore a variety of Thailand's beautiful natural scenery, both coastal and inland. With magnificent views ranging from white sand beaches to forests of mangroves, highlights of this four-hour circular route include: driving along Phuket Island's remote western coastline, crossing Sarasin Bridge to the mainland, visiting Wat Suwan Khuha and the Golden Reclining Buddha inside the legendary Monkey Caves …'"

"I've heard of that," Will interjected. "The Monkey Caves. Apparently, there are these monkeys who guard it, but instead of actually guarding it, they've just been trained to pickpocket tourists."

"Maybe we can pay 'em off in peanuts—protection fee," I said, scanning the rest of the description. "It looks like it also passes through some historic fishing villages and goes up to Phang Nga Bay, however you say that, which is famous for its limestone rock formations and sea caves and something called James Bond Island. Also, they have kayak rentals."

I looked up from the brochure. "That could be fun, to get up there and do some kayaking around the sea caves. We could even stay the night and then just drive back down here tomorrow."

"Monkeys and James Bond, sounds good to me," Will said, taking a bite of his omelet that had just arrived.

"And what about Jimmy?" I said after a moment, as much to myself as to Will.

Jimmy had stayed out even after Will and I had returned in the early hours, meaning there was no way of telling when he'd be up and, furthermore, when he did get up, what kind of condition he'd be in for taking a motorcycle trip … or even if he knew how to drive one, or even if he'd want to. Plus, of course, there was the fact that this could be the perfect opportunity to leave him behind. But then I thought about Will and Kelly and Shaun, West and Paddy, all the people who had instantly and unconditionally invited me into their lives over this past year, and I decided that that was who we were, the lifestyle I had signed up for.

"We could leave him a note," Will offered.

"No," I said. "We should wait. It wouldn't feel right leaving him behind."

"Leaving to go where?" a voice said from behind me.

I turned to see a disheveled Jimmy walking toward our table.

"Morning, Jimmy," I said. "We were just wondering how you fared last night."

Probably in part due to being hung over and in part to being caught off guard by what was the probably the warmest greeting I had yet given him, Jimmy seemed unsure of how to answer as he took a seat next to Will.

"Let's get you some orange juice and coffee," Will said.

Jimmy nodded in a way that looked as though he were in

pain.

Then, noticing the pamphlet on the table, he said, eyes half closed, "So what's this?"

"We were just talking about doing a motorcycle trip up the coast," Will said, looking at me.

"You're welcome to join," I said, giving Will a confirming smile, "if you're up for it. We'd head up today, do some sea kayaking, and come back tomorrow."

"I feel like shit," Jimmy said as he picked up the brochure, and for a moment, as he looked it over, it seemed as though he might decline. But then, shrugging, he added, "Yeah, why not. Those monkey caves sound kind of cool."

"They're guarded by pickpocketing monkeys, supposedly," I said, turning my smile into a smirk at Will.

Jimmy had closed his eyes again and held his head in his hands. "Little fuckers," he said without looking up.

***

As promised, the drive was gorgeous. For the first hour or so, we passed along miles of uninhabited coastline with only the occasional fishing village and roadside stand selling dried fish, squid, and gasoline as evidence of life. Then, once over the bridge, we began to head inland, driving through acres of mangroves, banana farms, cocoa plantations, and what Will, Mr. Trivia, identified as rubber trees, distinguished by the candy cane stripe that had been cut around their middles, apparently a mark left by the process of harvesting their milk. We stopped for a break of Thai iced tea, which was bright red in color and, like Thai coffee, flavored with sweetened condensed milk and served in plastic bags, then continued on under a thick canopy of green foliage, with temple spires standing out like mileposts and tribes of monkeys watching our passing like old folks on a porch. Opting to wait to go to the Monkey Caves until the next day, we continued ahead, up a steep hill and down the other side, soon passing shops, then harbors, and finally arriving at the bay.

Eager to get into the island-speckled water and cool off from the early afternoon heat, we followed a sandwich board advertising tours and rentals and wound up parking next to a souvenir stall selling headshots of Roger Moore posing as 007.

"Guess one of these is James Bond Island," I said, stretching my legs as I looked out at the massive rock formations jutting up out of the water. "One of the movies must have been filmed out here."

"License to kayak," Will said, standing and flexing his fingers. And, surprisingly, even though it was a pretty lame joke, I saw that this got a smile out of Jimmy, which in turn made me chuckle.

"Really?" Will said. "Not too cheesy?"

"Super cheesy," I said.

Jimmy shrugged but still looked amused.

"Alright, come on," I said, turning toward the shop.

* * *

"You won't have long inside," the woman at the kayak rental store told us. The air of humor we had enjoyed moments earlier had evaporated the instant we entered the shop. This, apparently, was serious business.

She looked at the wall clock.

"Two o'clock. So, leaving now, taking maybe one hour to get to a cave, you should not stay inside more than," she paused to make the calculations, "yes, not more than one hour. The tide comes in, the cave fills, the kayak cannot come out."

She pointed to a poster of a sea cave and indicated with her hand how the water would do the very thing she was describing. She looked back at us.

"You understand?"

We nodded, but she looked skeptical. She reminded me of a caricature of a strict schoolteacher, the kind you see in movies and comics.

"Yes," I said, always the diligent student, "we need to leave the cave before the water gets too high. By four o' clock."

"Mm. If you cannot come out, you must stay inside for the night. Sleep there, then come back in morning."

She paused then to give a little smile, but it didn't seem like she was kidding, especially when she added, "But this happens, and you must pay one day extra. Okay?"

We nodded again, and, apparently more convinced this time, she pointed out the places on the forms where we needed to sign.

This done, we placed our bags in the lockers and thanked her before setting out.

"Four o' clock, you must leave," she called out after us. "Do not forget."

* * *

After a little more than an hour of inexpertly paddling across open water and snaking around several of the promising giant mushroom-shaped rocks rising up out of the water around us, we finally settled on one to explore. The mouth of the cave was wide enough to fit two kayaks across, and there was a space of about ten or twelve feet from the top of the water to the cave ceiling above. It wasn't a huge opening, but it was certainly enough to pass through.

"Alright, you're the only one with a watch," I reminded

Will as Jimmy went gliding in ahead of us. "Better get us out by four."

"Don't want to spend the night in here, huh? Not your idea of romantic?"

It had begun getting darker once we entered the passageway, but I had a feeling he could take a pretty good guess at my expression.

We paddled toward the light at the end of the tunnel until, after a few minutes and maybe a distance of a hundred feet, we came out on the other side into a small open-air pool. Craggy rock walls of about sixty feet high surrounded us, and straight above was nothing but sky. The effect felt a bit like being at the bottom of a bowl or, I suppose, what it actually was: a long-ago erupted volcano. Beside us, there was a patch of ground just large enough to pull our kayaks onto, and I was surprised to see that it was even able to sustain the growth of a few small trees and bushes. Cut off from the rest of the world, surrounded by nothing but rock and salt water, these little things seemed to have defied the odds.

"I suppose we could survive on fish and learn to make fires from shrub branches if we were really desperate," Will said after we'd finished securing our kayaks and were having a look around at our mini plot of land.

"I'm sure you could," I said, looking away as Jimmy urinated against one of the walls.

Then, glancing around at the rock wall and seeing that someone had installed handgrips and a rope, I added, "Maybe we should go check out the view. Think we can make it?"

"We can see how far we get," Will said, and Jimmy agreed.

The three of us set out with Will in the lead, Jimmy following, and me bringing up the rear, and even without proper climbing gear, the going was fairly manageable. Trading off between using the rope and hand- and footholds, we continued on, steadily pulling our way up the wall, each at our own pace, for about twenty minutes.

I was about halfway up and the guys maybe three-fourths when Will called out, "Might be cutting it close. It's nearly three thirty."

Looking down, I could see that the water had, indeed, risen considerably. I returned my foot to the rock that I'd just stepped up from and was about to say that I was going to turn around when I heard Jimmy say, "We can make it. We're almost there."

"I don't know," Will said. "Honestly, sleeping in a bed does sound better than out here."

"Oh, come on," Jimmy called up toward Will, "you know they always tell people to be back earlier than you really need to be, just to cover their asses."

Will looked down at Jimmy and then at me, and I could see that he was debating whether or not to continue.

"How close are you?" I asked.

"Ten minutes," Will said, judging the remaining distance.

"Not even," Jimmy said.

"Go ahead," I said. "I'll just wait for you guys at the bottom. You can tell me if the view rivals Lijiang." I started climbing down, but then stopped and looked back up. "But, seriously, not much past four, okay? I don't want to have to leave you guys behind."

Will smiled. "You'd never," he said.

Naturally, I then spent the entire climb down thinking up contingency plans for if the guys actually didn't make it back in time. I considered whether it would be possible to pull their kayaks through and have them come down the other side. Or, if they came back down on this side, could they swim through the passageway? Could they hold their breath for a hundred feet? I imagined it'd be awfully dark.

I jumped down onto the small beach beside our kayaks and turned back to scan the top of the rock to see how far they'd gone. Seeing and hearing no one, I knew they'd made it to the top and glanced back at the cave mouth. There looked to be plenty of room still, so, taking a seat, I dangled my feet in the water and passed the time watching the fish nibble on the rocks below.

After another ten minutes or so, I stood and looked back up at the rock wall. There was still no sign of them. I looked at the cave again. There was a distance of about six feet left between the water and the rock ceiling. Still okay, but I'd feel better when I saw them climbing down.

Cupping my hands around my mouth, I called out Will's and then Jimmy's names a few times but received only an echo in response.

I sat back down but then almost immediately stood back up.

"Okay," I said aloud, turning toward the rocks. "Okay."

* * *

About halfway up, I took another look down at the cave mouth and hesitated. Maybe they *had* climbed down the other side. Maybe I *should* take the kayaks through … but something told me that that was wishful thinking. I knew Will wouldn't have left me, not intentionally. I just had to make it to the top and see, instead of continuing to run through the variety of scenarios created by my imagination. Somehow, they'd just gotten stuck, I kept telling myself. It'd be fine. There were three of us—we'd figure something out. And Will was strong. We could carry Jimmy down somehow, if that was the problem. That was probably it. I didn't want to blame Jimmy completely—he had grown on me a little, but he was still careless.

Irresponsible and inconsiderate. Will was none of those things. I wondered if Will would be upset at Jimmy. I'd never seen him angry before. He was always so … understanding. Kind. And funny. Smart. Thoughtful.

As these thoughts ran unimpeded through my head, I just kept moving, putting one hand in front of the other, boosting and pulling myself up until, at last, I reached the top.

And there, atop that ancient volcano, I saw no one.

Turning my head in every direction, I could see clearly around the surface of the rim, but it took a moment for me to stitch together what I was seeing into any kind of meaningful larger picture. Other than large, wet chunks of limestone rock jutting up at various angles, there was nothing but a few sparse shrubs. The outer edge overlooking the ocean lay about twenty feet ahead.

Bracing against the wind, I stood there, motionless, as a feeling came over me that all of this, all that was happening, had happened already. There seemed a futility in fighting against it, like I would no more be able to change the outcome here than I could the outcome of a movie. I could only watch what had already been written, accept the predestined.

But then I heard it. It could have been the call of a sea bird, but no, when it came again, I knew: it was a faint cry. Jarred out of my immobility, I rushed forward, losing my footing several times until, eventually by crawling, I arrived at the edge. Clinging to the rocks, trying to will myself to stop from shaking, I looked down.

There was so much water that at first it was all I could see. Blue and white and alive. Other rock formations rose up in the distance, but below, sixty feet straight down, there were only waves. Hearing another cry, this one only briefly before it was cut off with a sickening gurgle, I scanned the water. I moved my gaze to the right around the base of the rock, and there I saw Jimmy, a dark purple circle seeping out into the water around him. He pawed limply at the water, struggling to keep his head above the surface.

Scanning again, I moved my search to the left, but this time, there was no sound or labored movement. There was only Will, being pushed by the waves up against the rock base.

Once, in college, a few friends and I drove an hour out to a spot we'd heard about on the river. An abandoned train trestle ran across it, and if you went to the middle—and, in my case, didn't look straight down before you jumped—you'd be fine. It was only fifty feet down, but in the air, it felt like forever. This was what flashed through my mind as I took another quick scan below, then stood, secured my footing, looked straight out, and jumped.

My feet hit first, and the bottoms of my soles stung and continued stinging even after my momentum had ceased carrying me downward and I had flailed and kicked my way back up to the surface. For a moment, it was only this: the stinging in my feet and a ringing in my ears. But soon I was aware of the waves, pushing me down from above, and I turned in search of something to help orient myself. Behind me, close and big, loomed the wall of the rock formation, but with its mushroom shape, narrower at the base with a rocky overhang above, there was nothing to hang on to. So instead, I kicked, trying to propel myself upward, to see above the choppy water. And then, again, I heard something and swam toward it, head down, eyes open in a cloud of salty water.

I saw Jimmy slipping just beneath the water and, grabbing him underneath the arms, pulled him to the surface. He breathed, a strange raspy breath, but it was enough. Wrapping one of my arms around his chest while freeing up the other, I began paddling again in the direction of the cave mouth, toward where I had seen Will.

I found him just as he was when I had spotted him from above, and pulling him away from the rocks and turning him over, I saw that his face was drained of color save for a deep red gash across the side of his head.

Unthinkingly, I let go of Jimmy and grabbed Will's head and tried breathing several times into his mouth. But there was nothing, no sign of life, and beside me Jimmy began sinking again beneath the water. I held on to Will, unable to let go, until I felt Jimmy's panicked arm brush against mine.

"Hold still!" I yelled at him as I grabbed his head with one hand and held it above water. Incredibly, he obeyed. I could see he had a large gash, too; his was on one side of his torso and was bleeding badly. Despite the relentlessness of the waves, I could now see the real reason for his sudden compliance: he had gone unconscious.

With both arms occupied, and knowing that I would be unable to support the three of us for much longer by kicking alone, I yelled and searched for help, but there was none. Then, because I needed to do something, I hooked an arm around Will and began pulling him toward the entrance of the cave. After a few seconds, I left him and returned for the now-unresponsive Jimmy. I did this several times, taking it in turns to pull both Jimmy and Will closer to the cave, but each time, I returned just as the other began slipping beneath the water.

Looking down into the long dark corridor ahead, I saw that there was now less than two feet of space between the top of the water and the jagged rocks of the cave ceiling above. With one more look at Will, colorless, motionless, lifeless, I tightened an arm around Jimmy's chest and plunged into the cave.

Trying to avoid scraping our heads and arms against the sharp rocks above, I navigated us through the tunnel, moving forward toward the light, until finally we arrived on the other side. I hauled Jimmy up onto the small patch of remaining ground and clumsily began attempting to perform CPR. One, two, three, four, five, six … I tried to remember the training I had received a few years earlier when I had taken first aid as part of a summer job working at a daycare, but just before reaching the thirty requisite compressions, Jimmy sputtered. Rolling him onto his side, I then jumped up and unfastened one of the kayaks.

"We've got to go," I said, not waiting for him to acknowledge or comprehend his surroundings. Pulling him over to the kayak, I lifted his head and upper body into the seat and draped his legs across the top. "Just don't move," I added as I strung the lead rope around myself. Without another thought, I plunged back into the dark water.

The going was even slower now, with the kayak and Jimmy's knees bumping and snagging against the rocks, and when I stopped to catch my breath, turning over onto my back for a moment, my nose felt just inches from the cave ceiling. It was too dark to see, but it smelled of dead things, like the shells and seaweed my siblings and I would collect from the beach when we were kids and would find again the next day, sitting in the plastic bag where we had left them.

When we finally emerged, Will was gone.

* * *

A tour boat had spotted Jimmy and me at some point on our way back toward shore. Once on board, I tried to tell them what happened, but nothing seemed to make sense.

"A climbing accident," I heard one of the passengers relay to another. He was speaking in English. A foreigner.

Someone, perhaps the captain, was at the radio, speaking

in Thai.

"Climbing? Out here?" another passenger responded.

I sat on the deck while they attended to Jimmy, who could only moan and cough.

"They're not sure how many are missing. At least one. These two seem to be in shock."

"Here comes Search and Rescue."

I saw a speedboat, its lights and siren signaling the arrival.

"Can you tell them where you last saw him? Is it just one person?"

"Yes," I said, looking out over the water. Several large rocks dotted the horizon. "He's alone. But I don't know where."

* * *

An ambulance was waiting to take the two of us to the hospital. I told them I had to look for Will, but a Thai police officer ushered me into the back of the ambulance behind Jimmy's gurney.

"Will Carmichael," I said. "We can't leave him."

The police officer waved his hand to stop me from getting out and shut the door.

At the hospital, after being escorted into a room and evaluated briefly, I was left by myself. Then, after an amount of time I had no way of knowing, another police officer and a translator entered my room, and I told the story over again, as much of it as I could.

I didn't know what had happened at the top. I hadn't seen it happen, I explained—they had fallen before I got there—but the rocks were slippery. Plus, it was windy, really windy. I could feel that it sounded as though I were making excuses, even as I talked, but it mattered to me that they didn't think of Will as careless. Or reckless. He was neither of those things.

He was young and spontaneous, but in a responsible way. The whole thing, the motorcycles, the kayaking, the cave, they had all been my idea in the first place. None of this was Will's fault.

"How did you get down?"

I wasn't sure if the translator had cut me off or had just interrupted my thoughts.

"I saw they were injured, so I jumped in after them to help."

"And you were injured also?"

I looked around at my limbs and body. A new bandage had appeared around my knee.

"Maybe I hit my knee," I said.

The translator said something to the officer, then turned back to me.

"No guide?" he asked.

"No."

The two of them talked together again.

"We understand," the translator said after a minute. "The three of you rented kayaks but went on your own, climbed the rock, and two fell from the top by accident, one jumped after to save the two who had fallen. In the end, there were two injuries, one fatality. We will have some papers for you to sign later, okay?"

I nodded as the officer said something else.

"You are all Americans?" the translator reiterated.

"Yes."

"We will need your passports."

"They're in the lockers," I said, just remembering. "At the rental shop."

They nodded and left.

I sat alone again, this time for what felt like hours, until a new doctor came in and asked how I was doing. He was

German, I could tell by his accent, but spoke fluent English.

He told me that my friend would be all right: he'd broken an arm and two ribs, and his side had been stitched up, his stomach pumped of seawater.

"What about Will?" I asked. "The other one?"

The doctor hesitated.

"They are still looking, I heard," he said. "I think you will stay here, and maybe there will be news in the morning."

I nodded, and the doctor waited another moment.

"Your knee needs stitches," he said.

I nodded again.

He poked his head out into the hall and said something in Thai. A nurse came in, then left again after being told something. She soon returned with supplies.

Once she unwrapped the bandage, I could see that it was another deep cut. I had no memory of how I might have gotten it—on one of the rocks at the top? when I jumped? swimming through the cave? I felt nothing, but, seeing it now, I did think about how odd it looked. In combination with the other two scars, it seemed almost to form the perfect shape of an X.

When they finished stitching it, the nurse re-wrapped it and left.

"There's a room with beds," the doctor said. "A nurse will take you there, and you can stay the night."

"Thanks," I said. "I'm not sure what I'm supposed to do."

"You are American?" he asked.

I nodded. This preoccupation with nationality also struck me.

"I will tell reception to call the consulate. I think they will help you."

"Okay, thanks," I repeated.

After the doctor left, the nurse returned and walked me

down a hallway. We passed by a room with an open door, and I saw Jimmy lying on a bed, eyes closed, with a splint wrapped around his arm. There were two empty chairs beside his bed.

I kept following the nurse, and she pointed me into the next room, where there were four empty beds. I thanked her, but when she left, I took a blanket off of one of the beds and limped silently back toward Jimmy's room. Seeing that he was asleep, I pushed the chairs together, curled up in them, and covered myself with the blanket. It was quiet, other than the sound of his breathing.

I must have eventually fallen asleep because sometime in the morning, Jimmy and I were both awakened by a nurse telling us that someone was here for us. I looked at Jimmy, but neither of us said anything. I stood and followed the nurse back out into the hall where a man in a suit was waiting.

For the next half an hour, seated in the waiting room's plastic chairs, the man, American, from the consulate, asked me questions, business-like, professional.

Was there someone they should notify?

I began writing down the name and contact information for my parents, but then reconsidered. There wasn't anything they could do at the moment; they didn't know where I was, and they didn't know Will or his family. A call from the consulate would only cause confusion and worry; I would talk to them later. But for Will ... I had never met his father. I knew his name was Martin and that he owned a construction company in Pittsburgh. I doubted any of this was helpful. His number would probably be saved in Will's phone, but the phones and passports were either still in the lockers or, if they had been retrieved, the police may have taken them. I decided to put Roger's name and the name of the restaurant down instead. I didn't know anything about Jimmy's family. Though he had signed his name and contact information on the moped and kayak rental papers, I had never taken notice.

"Just call Roger," I said, pointing to the name I had written down. "He'll be at the restaurant, The Foreign Burrito, in Kunming, China. He can call Will's father or give you the number. I'd like to talk to him, too—Roger, I mean—if I can. Where will we go from here?"

"They found the body early this morning. The medical examiner will take a look today, so you'll likely be cleared to leave custody soon. We'll help the two of you get into a hotel this afternoon, and you can stay there while we wait to hear from the police."

They had found Will.

"Our lives … the apartment …" I wasn't sure what I wanted to ask or say. "Everything's in China."

"I would suggest going back to the U.S. once you can travel, until everything gets sorted out. But it will be up to you."

"Okay," I said.

"I think that's everything," the man said. "I'll call this Roger person and put you in touch with him. But it would be best if you avoided communicating with too many people. And stay away from the press. My guess is you'll have to stay in town for a few days, maybe a week."

When the man got up and went outside, I stayed where I was.

They had found Will. And, soon, people would know. This man would be telling Roger in a matter of minutes. Roger would tell Mei. Then everyone at the bar—they'd have to plan a service. Not to mention his family and friends back home. They would be going about their business, perhaps for another few hours, happily unaware of the sudden hole that had just ripped open in the lives of all who loved him.

The man returned with a phone.

"Here's Roger."

The man left to talk to someone at reception, and I put the phone to my ear. At the sound of Roger's voice, I began to sob.

Eventually, Roger said he would make the calls and the necessary arrangements. We both said we'd see each other soon, but neither with any conviction.

I handed the phone back to the consulate officer, and he said he'd be in touch. He reiterated that we should stay here until he returned.

I walked back to Jimmy's room, but with a nurse and doctor in there attending to him, I turned at the door and went into my room instead. I chose the bed that I had removed the blanket from, and sat on it. I suddenly realized that I was still in my kayaking clothes—shorts and a tank top over a swimsuit—and sandals. No passport, no money, severely underprepared to be stuck here for a week … severely underprepared to fly home. I thought about the business card that had led to my rescue last time and the one person who I wanted to be here, who wasn't.

Shutting my eyes tight, all I could think was, *Please, Will, don't be gone.*

* * *

The police officer and translator returned early in the afternoon and came into our respective rooms to talk to us individually, first to Jimmy and then to me. It was an accident, they concluded—no fault. According to Jimmy, he had slipped, Will had lunged to grab him, and off balance due to the wet rocks, they had both fallen over the edge. The medical report showed that Will died from a head wound consistent with a fall. They had spoken with the U.S. consulate officer, and nothing more was needed from us. We were free to go. The driver would take us soon.

I asked about our passports and bags left at the kayak shop.

The consulate officer would have our things.

I signed something, and they left.

The consulate officer returned shortly thereafter. He brought our bags, including Will's, and confirmed what the police had said. If we were ready, he would help us get to a nearby guesthouse and book tickets to Bangkok for as soon as we could fly. From there, he said, we could change our original return flights to go wherever we needed.

After signing some insurance papers and statements, I went back to check on Jimmy.

"Are you leaving?" he asked when I appeared in his doorway. He looked groggy, like he was on painkillers. His arm now lay in a bulky cast and sling in front of him.

"We'll go together, when the doctor says you can leave. First to a hotel for a few days, and then flying to Bangkok."

"Okay," he said.

"They brought our bags, so we can change before we leave."

He nodded.

"They brought our phones and our passports, too. I'll work on changing our tickets. I'll need your info, but that can wait."

I had turned to go, but when I glanced back at him, I saw that he had started to cry. And though something in me wanted to rush forward, shake him, scream at him that he had no right, something else held me back.

After a moment of silence, instead of doing or saying any of the things I felt, I said only, "It'll be okay."

It seemed like something Will would have said, and, right then, I didn't have the heart for anything else.

EPILOGUE

~ Coming Back ~

I do not bring back from a jouney
... the same self that I took.
—W. Somerset Maugham

Hilo, Hawaii, October 2019—It's autumn now. There are no changing leaves and the temperature's about the same as it is all year round, but after six years I think I'm finally starting to recognize the seasons. A few hours less of sunlight, a few inches more of rain, another term underway. It's a nice afternoon, though, and as I step out of my department building, I take in the scene: the lawn, per usual, has been taken over by students, some playing frisbee, some napping, others chatting or listening to music; orange and black posters detailing plans for a Halloween party dot the surrounding lampposts; and a row of carved pumpkins lines the walkway to the library. It really is a beautiful campus, a perfect place to write, I think as I set down my satchel full of papers to be graded and take a seat on one of the nearby benches. Palm trees sway all around us, and in every direction, the view is green, lush, and living. It reminds me of Kunming in many ways, that eternal state of spring. I think of that first run to the park, Green Lake, the weeping willows and the music, elderly Chinese dancing in step. And I think, too, of the scroll, now hanging in my office, the lake, as green in the painting as in real life, the pagoda against a blue sky, the white and red cherry blossoms. A moment in time, forever unchanged.

I sit for a few more minutes, laptop at the ready, then take out my phone and snap a picture of the pumpkins. The detail on some of them is incredible, and it almost seems a shame how quickly they will wither in this humidity. But I suppose that's the way with everything. And it's for us to work out which images to cling to, to see past the scars and decay, and remember all the rest, the impact, the detail, the fullness, and the beauty of a life lived.

I move the cursor down to the end of the story and type out a Chinese poem by Li Bai I had translated:

You ask me why I dwell on the green mountain.
I smile but do not answer, my soul rests in peace.
As the peach blossom flows downstream on the river
and disappears forever into the unknown,
so I am taken beyond this world of men, to heaven.

Then, with an exhale, I close my laptop and stand. *Time to go back*, I think, grabbing my satchel and turning toward home, tether intact and feeling something close to peace.